Megastar Mysteries

Fusion

Annabelle Starr

EGMONT

Special thanks to:

Rachel Rimmer, St John's Walworth Church of England
School and Belmont Primary School

EGMONT

We bring stories to life

Published in Great Britain 2007
by Egmont UK Limited
239 Kensington High Street, London W8 6SA

Text & illustrations © 2007 Egmont UK Ltd
Text by Rachel Rimmer
Illustrations by Helen Turner

The moral rights of the author and illustrator have been asserted

ISBN 978 1 4052 3243 2

1 3 5 7 9 10 8 6 4 2

A CIP catalogue record for this title is available
from the British Library

Typeset by Avon DataSet Ltd, Bidford on Avon, Warwickshire
Printed and bound in Great Britain by the CPI Group

'I like a bit of a mystery, so I thought it was very good'
Phoebe, age 10

'I liked the way there's stuff about modelling and
make-up, cos that's what girls like'
Beth M, age 11

'Great idea – very cool! Not for boys . . .'
Louise, age 9

'I really enjoyed reading the books. They keep
you on your toes and the characters are really interesting
(I love the illustrations!) . . . They balance out humour
and suspense'
Beth R, age 10

'Exciting and quite unpredictable. I like that the girls
do the detective work'
Lauren, age 10

'All the characters are very realistic. I would definitely
recommend these to a friend'
Krystyna, age 9

We want to know what *you* think about
Megastar Mysteries! Visit:

www.mega-star.co.uk

for loads of coolissimo megastar
stuff to do!

Meet the
Megastar Mysteries Team!

Hi, this is me, **Rosie Parker** (otherwise known as Nosy Parker), and these are my best mates . . .

. . . **Soph** (Sophie) **McCoy** - she's a real fashionista sista - and . . .

. . . **Abs** (Abigail) **Flynn**, who's officially une grande genius.

Here's my mum, **Liz Parker**. Much to my embarrassment, her fashion and music taste is well and truly stuck in the 1980s (but despite all that I still love her dearly) . . .

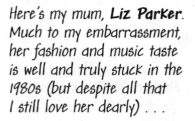

. . . and my nan, **Pam Parker**, the murder-mystery freak I mentioned on the cover. Sometimes, just sometimes, her crackpot ideas do come in handy.

Consider yourself introduced!

Rosie's Mini Megastar Phrasebook

Want to speak our lingo, but don't know your soeurs from your signorinas? No problemo! Just use my comprehensive guide . . .

-a-rama	add this ending to a word to indicate a large quantity: e.g. 'The after-show party was celeb-a-rama'
amigo	Spanish for 'friend'
au contraire, mon frère	French for 'on the contrary, my brother'
au revoir	French for 'goodbye'
barf/barfy/barfissimo	sick/sick-making/very sick-making indeed
bien sûr, ma soeur	French for 'of course, my sister'
bon	French for 'good'
bonjour	French for 'hello'
celeb	short for 'celebrity'
convo	short for 'conversation'
cringe-fest	a highly embarrassing situation
Cringeville	a place we all visit from time to time when something truly embarrassing happens to us
cringeworthy	an embarrassing person, place or thing might be described as this
daggy	Australian for 'unfashionable' or unstylish'
doco	short for 'documentary'
exactamundo	not a real foreign word, but a great way to express your agreement with someone
exactement	French for 'exactly'

excusez moi	French for 'excuse me'
fashionista	'a keen follower of fashion' – can be teamed with 'sista' for added rhyming fun
glam	short for 'glamorous'
gorge/gorgey	short for 'gorgeous': e.g. 'the lead singer of that band is gorge/gorgey'
hilarioso	not a foreign word at all, just a great way to liven up 'hilarious'
hola, señora	Spanish for 'hello, missus'
hottie	no, this is *not* short for hot water bottle – it's how you might describe an attractive-looking boy to your friends
-issimo	try adding this ending to English adjectives for extra emphasis: e.g. coolissimo, crazissimo – très funissimo, non?
je ne sais pas	French for 'I don't know'
je voudrais un beau garçon, s'il vous plaît	French for 'I would like an attractive boy, please'
journos	short for 'journalists'
les Français	French for, erm, 'the French'
Loserville	this is where losers live, particularly evil school bully Amanda Hawkins
mais	French for 'but'
marvelloso	not technically a foreign word, just a more exotic version of 'marvellous'
massivo	Italian for 'massive'
mon amie/mes amis	French for 'my friend'/'my friends'
muchos	Spanish for 'many'

non	French for 'no'
nous avons deux garçons ici	French for 'we have two boys here'
no way, José!	'that's never going to happen!'
oui	French for 'yes'
quelle horreur!	French for 'what horror!'
quelle surprise!	French for 'what a surprise!'
sacré bleu	French for 'gosh' or even 'blimey'
stupido	this is the Italian for 'stupid' – stupid!
-tastic	add this ending to any word to indicate a lot of something: e.g. 'Abs is braintastic'
très	French for 'very'
swoonsome	decidedly attractive
si, si, signor/signorina	Italian for 'yes, yes, mister/miss'
terriblement	French for 'terribly'
une grande	French for 'a big' – add the word 'genius' and you have the perfect description of Abs
Vogue	it's only the world's most influential fashion magazine, darling!
voilà	French for 'there it is'
what's the story, Rory?	'what's going on?'
what's the plan, Stan?	'which course of action do you think we should take?'
what the crusty old grandads?	'what on earth?'
zut alors!	French for 'darn it!'

Hi Megastar reader!

My name's Annabelle Starr*. I'm a fashion stylist – just like Soph's Aunt Penny – which means it's my job to help celebrities look their best at all times.

Over the years, I've worked with all sorts of big names, some of whom also have seriously big egos! Take the time I flew all the way to Japan to style a shoot for a girl band. One of the members refused to wear the designer number I'd picked out for her and insisted on sporting a dress her mum had run up from some revolting old curtains instead. The only way I could get her to take it off was to persuade her it didn't match her pet Pekinese's outfit!

Anyway, when I first started out, I never dreamt I'd write a series of books based around my crazy celebrity experiences, but that's just what I've done with Megastar Mysteries. Rosie, Soph and Abs have just the sort of adventures I wish my friends and I could have got up to when we were teenagers!

I really hope you enjoy reading the books as much as I enjoyed writing them!

Love **Annabelle**

* I'll let you in to a little secret: this isn't my real name, but in this business you can never be too careful!

Chapter One

I couldn't believe we were going on holiday to Smallhampton. For a *fortnight*. I mean, it was bad enough when Abs and Soph were both away at half-term, but at least that was only for a week. Now I had to cope for two weeks without them! In a *holiday park*. Me, Rosie Parker, friend to the stars – well, OK, one star – in a holiday park! Quelle horreur!

I was stunned when Mum told me where we were going.

'It'll be fun, Rosie,' she said, coming into my

room with an armload of washing. 'I chose a really great place. It's got a disco and everything.' Then she started giggling for some reason.

I just looked at her like she was a mad woman. Then it clicked. *Oh, no. Knowing Mum, she's probably booked the one holiday park that only has eighties music for entertainment. Nightmare!*

'Mum, for the last time, I do not want to dance to Wham! with you!' I said, rolling my eyes.

'Now *that* was a great band,' she said, smiling wistfully as she left the room.

I thought about what she'd said. She was right – there could be some cute boys there. That would make up for two weeks in the middle of nowhere, away from my best friends.

Yeah, well, that's what I thought . . . until Soph invited me and Abs to stay with her in France! Soph's family are mega-rich – well, richer than me and Mum and Nan, anyway – and they were hiring a really big villa near the coast, with a pool. Soph said it was like one of those places you see on *MTV Cribs*, with really large rooms and flowers everywhere, and a pool table and a fully stocked fridge (which you know the celeb never touches, because they're on some crazy diet or something, and they've got a personal chef anyway). I was *so* desperate to go. We would get a tan for a start, and there would be French boys there. I could practise my Français: 'Bonjour! Une baguette, s'il vous plaît.' You see, I'm a natural!

That day, Soph and Abs and I spent all of French class getting the phrase 'un beau garçon' into every conversation, which really annoyed Madame Bertillon:

Soph: *Bonjour. Je voudrais un beau garçon, s'il vous plaît.*
Moi: *Oui, oui. Nous avons deux garçons ici . . .*
Madame Bertillon *(in that sort of growly bark she does):* Girls! You're supposed to be in a bakery!
Amanda Hawkins *(my arch-enemy):* Yeah, duh.

We had brilliant plans. We'd even decided to colour-coordinate our bikinis and nail varnish. OK, Soph had decided that. But then Mum went and put a dampener on the whole thing.

'But Rosie, I've already booked the holiday park for those weeks,' she said. 'I can't cancel it now. I'm sorry, love, but you can't go to France.'

I couldn't believe it. She was spoiling everything. 'But Mum . . .'

'I'm sorry, Rosie. But I'm not going to ruin our family holiday just because you and your friends want to swan off together. You see enough of them as it is. I'm sure you'll survive for two weeks without them.'

TWO WEEKS ALONE! I'D BE A SOCIAL OUTCAST!

We had an emergency meeting at Abs's house.

'Did you try flattery?' suggested Abs helpfully. 'Y'know, like she might meet a nice man without you cramping her style?'

'Yep.'

'Did you try bribery?' asked Soph.

'And sulking and shouting and all that. But I still have to go.' I sighed. 'I can't believe you two are going to be in France without me.'

We all sighed.

For the next three weeks, Abs and Soph were really brilliant. They managed not to talk about it in front of me, but I could tell they were really excited about the sun, and the pool, and the French boys . . .

They came round to say goodbye the day we left. Soph had brought some nail varnish with her, to decorate my wellies. They looked *quite cool* once she'd finished, actually, even though I wouldn't have chosen blue frogs myself. That's Soph for you. Always ahead of the fashion game.

'You laugh now, my friend,' she said, 'but you wait. In a few months' time, customised wellies will be in all the fashion mags. Just think of all those celebs who go to festivals. What do they wear? Wellies!'

'Yeah, but blue frogs?' I said.

'Hey, you will text us the whole time, won't

you?' said Abs, changing the subject. 'And we'll have broadband at the villa, so we can instant message each other, too.'

'Bien sûr, ma soeur. *If* there's a computer. I'll be so bored, I'll be bothering you, like, every hour. In fact, I'll be so bored I might even look at that play we're supposed to read for drama. I've packed it, just in case.'

'Wow.' Soph was impressed. 'Mr Lord will love you. Maybe he'll make you the lead in the play next term.'

'Yeah, right,' I said. 'Like Time Lord will *ever* spot my star potential.'

'Rosie!' Nan called up the stairs. 'Time to go!'

I sighed, rolled my eyes and trudged out of my room. Abs and Soph trailed behind me, both doing a very good job of looking sad.

Nan was waiting in the hall. 'Have fun, girls!' she trilled to Abs and Soph. 'Don't go doing anything I wouldn't do!'

'Like what?' they asked.

This was normally the cue for Nan to start

warning them about strange men or over-friendly new neighbours who could be up to no good, but we were saved by a shout from Mum. She was in the sitting room, where she was trying to sort out the satellite TV.

'I think it's broken!' she called.

'What?!' Nan was horrified. She trotted into the sitting room to check out the awful truth. 'It can't be! What about the *Murder Mystery Weekend* special? I won't be able to record it!'

I could sympathise with Nan. We were both being torn from the things (or people) we loved – in my case, the girls and my whole life; in her case, the TV with its many, many, *many* murder-mystery shows. Nan loves them. Particularly *Murder, She Wrote*. Angela Lansbury – the actress who plays Jessica Fletcher, the writer–detective – is her favourite. I don't know why. Personally, I think it's really dodgy that a murder happens wherever Jessica goes. But Nan thinks she's brilliant. 'Watch and learn, Rosie, watch and learn,' she says. It's amazing I ever get to watch *EastEnders* or *Big*

Brother, or anything, really, considering how she hogs the TV.

Anyway, Mum had decided we all did too much telly-watching. Although there would be a TV at this park, she was planning to limit how much we could watch. 'We should be getting out there and meeting people,' she said, 'not getting square eyes in front of the telly.'

Nan was not happy. Especially because the *Murder Mystery Weekend* special started right when we were supposed to be driving to this holiday park. The Satellite TV was her new toy and her lifeline.

'I'm sorry, Mother, but I can't work this blooming thing out,' Mum said. 'Rosie, you're better at it than I am. Come and fix it, please. But remember we have to leave in ten minutes.'

'Er, Rosie, we've gotta go,' said Soph. 'Soz.'

'We'll call you,' said Abs. 'Promise.'

I grabbed them and hugged them close. It was going to be a *long* two weeks. Then, sighing again, I trudged into the sitting room. Even my dramatic parting from Soph and Abs had been ruined.

Just a few hours later, I was feeling like I'd been travelling to Smallhampton for my whole *life*. It didn't help that my mum insisted on playing Bananarama songs most of the way. Like, who even cares about them now? Mum, that's who. She warbled along to their track 'Robert De Niro's Waiting' as she sped round a roundabout, making me and Nan lurch sideways.

'*Mum!*' I pleaded.

'Oh, sorry, Rosie. How about we put something of yours on instead? Something by that Mirage Muggins? Is that better? More trendy?'

Honestly. I wonder about her sanity sometimes. What hope do I have? Especially when you consider I'm related to Nan, too, who spent the whole car journey muttering about the satellite TV. Thank goodness for mobiles. I spent most of the journey texting things like 'Help!' and 'got 2 get outta here' to Soph and Abs. And compiling this list:

Top ten reasons why going on holiday with my family is really annoying:

1. The music in the car. For every Mirage Mullins song I'm allowed to play, we have to have an eighties 'classic'. Oh, what I'd do for an MP3 player . . .

2. Stopping for a wee and a cup of tea every few miles. Nan loves checking out every service-station toilet and how clean it is. Plus, she can't cope without a cuppa for very long. I have tried to point out that I can't cope without an injection of cash for very long, but Mum has failed to get the hint.

3. At this holiday park, I will be stuck in the middle of nowhere, with no friends and no shops. Aaargh!

4. I'll probably be forced to take part in organised activities like crazy golf . . . or darts . . . or dance classes. Actually, if the dance classes get you to dance like the celebs on *Strictly Come Dancing*, that would be cool.

Apart from the spangly shirts they make the men wear. But I bet this place will have eighties dance classes, where you wear really gross leotards and legwarmers. Mum's idea of heaven!

5. I'm sooo not going to meet anyone famous there.

6. I know Abs and Soph will have loads of fun without me. And meet sexy French boys.

7. I may be so bored I have to do some homework.

8. I have to put up with Nan moaning about missing the *Murder Mystery Weekend* special.

9. There probably won't be anyone my age there, and I'll be forced to make friends with old ladies and young boys who are in the Scouts.

10. It's for a whole *fortnight*!

So, basically, by the time we got to the holiday park, we were all a bit miserable. Mum was trying to be in a good mood, but even she had been ground down by Nan's muttering, and my heavy, dramatic sighs.

It was getting dark as we pulled in through the gates, down the track that took us to reception. I could see lots of lodges that were supposed to look like log cabins. They all had cars next to them. It seemed to be a popular place. I just hoped it was popular with cool people.

Mum went into reception to say we'd arrived, and while Nan went to find a toilet, I wandered through to the restaurant area. The yellow plastic chairs and laminated tables that were fixed to the ground reminded me of the school canteen. I shuddered.

Then I caught sight of a poster on the wall. It listed the entertainment for the week, so I went over for a closer look. *Best to get the bad news over with in one go.*

To my surprise, it actually looked quite cool. There was some band called Fusion playing all fortnight, and they looked really good from the photo! The girls were wearing funky clothes, and one of the boys was seriously cute. He had a guitar slung round his neck, and was holding a microphone, looking really cool. He had dark wavy hair and piercing blue eyes. I know it sounds weird, but I felt like he was staring back at me as I stood gazing at the poster.

Fusion. It sounded a bit familiar. Maybe I'd read something about them somewhere? It said they were 'up-and-coming' on the poster. Wouldn't it be cool if I saw them play just before they shot to mega-fame?!

'Rosie? Rosie! Oh, there you are!' said Mum, coming in to the 'restaurant'. 'Come on, I've got the keys. We're in number forty-two. Where's your nan?'

'Loo,' I said automatically, as I followed Mum out. With a hot band like Fusion hanging around the place, maybe this holiday was going to be a tiny bit interesting after all . . .

Chapter Two

Unfortunately, while Mum was at reception, she'd discovered there was a nightly karaoke event in the bar and signed herself up for it. She announced this over breakfast on the first morning. 'So I thought I'd start with "Holiday" by Madonna – you know, because we're on holiday. And then I'd move on to a Bananarama song – don't know which one yet – and then I'd finish with "Lady in Red". What do you reckon?'

I looked at her in horror. 'You're not serious, Mum? You're going to do this to me on our first night here? In front of everyone?'

'Oh, come on, Rosie. It'll be fun!' she said.

I had to get out of there. The lodge was OK, actually. I had my own room, thank goodness, and Nan had decided it was clean enough for her (which was saying something), but I couldn't stand one more minute with my insane relatives. I decided to go and check out the magazines in the shop. I was praying they'd have some celebrity gossip. Anything, really, that would take my mind off the horror that is my mum singing.

It was a nice day, and despite everything I was quite chirpy as I walked to the shop. I hadn't seen anyone my age yet, but I was sure that not *all* the happy holiday-parkers would be nans and eighties enthusiasts. Would they?

The shop was pretty well stocked. They had all the latest issues of the essential mags. I was browsing through them when the door opened and a load of people walked in. This girl squeezed past me, and I looked up.

It was one of the members of Fusion! She had

blonde hair with streaks in it and was wearing a pink-and-green dress over some baggy jeans, with a pair of bright red clogs. It looked weird, but cool-weird. A bit like Soph, actually. Which is maybe why I said 'Hi!' in a très familiar way, before really thinking about what I was saying.

'Er, hi!' she said, clearly wondering if she knew me.

'Um, I saw you on a poster last night,' I gabbled. 'You're in that band, right?'

'Yeah,' she smiled. 'That's right. Fusion. My name's Ella.'

'I'm Rosie,' I said.

'Hey, is that the issue with Chad and Cheryl's wedding in it?' she asked, pointing at my magazine.

'Yeah.' I showed her. 'I can't believe he wore a pink suit with a black shirt! I mean, he looks terrible! How can someone so fit look totally awful at his own wedding?!'

'I know!' she said. 'Cheryl looks all right, but her bridesmaids? Er, hel-*lo*? Why are they wearing *orange*?!'

'Ah, well, orange is the colour that says "Don't look at me – look at the bride." It's a well-known fact,' I said knowledgeably. I hadn't spent my entire life reading glossy magazines for nothing.

Ella laughed. Just then, another girl shouted, 'Hi! I'm Lauren!' right in my ear. She had really, really long dark hair in a ponytail and a really, really loud voice.

'Er, hi!' I said, leaning back from her and wincing slightly. 'I'm Rosie.'

'Hi, Rosie!' she roared, twirling her ponytail as she spoke. 'Have you been staying here long?'

'No, we arrived last night.' I tried to step away from her for the sake of my ears, but squished myself against the magazine rack instead.

'So did we,' said Ella. She yawned, and smiled. 'We're playing here for a fortnight. Can't believe we're here, actually, but our manager said it would be good for our profile. And Maff over there seemed keen to come.' She nodded towards the back of the shop as if to point out this Maff person.

'Wow, you have a manager!' I said, in a totally not-cool way. 'So are you, like, famous? Could you be in one of these magazines?'

'Not yet!' Lauren shouted. 'But hopefully soon!' She grinned at me, and I grinned back nervously. *Why is she shouting?!*

'Don't mind Lauren. She always shouts,' Ella said softly. 'She's our drummer and she's a bit deaf.'

'What?' Lauren yelled.

Then my heart stopped as I saw the cute boy from the poster approaching us.

'Hey, what are you girls doing?' he asked. He was wearing really baggy jeans and very cool trainers, and his blue T-shirt totally matched his eyes! *How* gorge?!

'This is Rosie,' said Ella. 'She just got here, like us. Rosie, this is Maff. He plays guitar and sings.'

I gulped, and my hand shot out towards him without me telling it to. He smiled, raising an eyebrow, then slowly shook my hand. 'Hi,' he said. 'Nice to meet you.'

'Nice to meet you, too,' I managed to say. 'Gosh. Maff. That's an unusual name. Is it short for something?' *Stop it, Rosie! Stop it! Way to totally unimpress a cute boy. Could you be any more boring?*

Luckily, he laughed. 'Yeah, short for Matthew. But even my mum calls me Maff now.'

Wow, his eyes are amazing, I thought. I was totally staring at him and all I could think was, *Why did I just throw on my worst pair of shorts this morning? I must look awful.*

'Hey, listen,' said Ella. 'Since it's our first night here, we're having a sort of mini party after our gig, to celebrate. We've got to rehearse now, but why don't we meet up later?'

'What?' I said, still staring at Maff. 'Oh, yeah, cool! So what's the plan, Stan?'

'We're playing in the American diner!' yelled Lauren. 'You know, next to the restaurant with the bright yellow chairs! After our set, we're gonna have hamburgers and fries, and dance like we're in *Grease!*' She started bopping about in a really silly way. She still looked cool. Maybe just being in a band gives you instant coolness, no matter what you do.

Ella smiled at me, and Maff raised his eyebrow again.

'Great!' I said. 'See you there.'

Wow! I was going out with a nearly-famous band that night!

* * *

Ten outfit changes later and I still wasn't happy with what I was wearing. I'd texted Abs and Soph pictures of me in various looks. Soph had made some really good suggestions, but I still wasn't convinced. I really wanted to look cool to impress the band.

I'd found the holiday-park computer room earlier, so I was able to instant message the girls about what had happened. Oh, and I'd done a bit of research on Fusion too.

NosyParker: Guess what?!!!
CutiePie: What?

FashionPolice: Everyone loves your frog wellies?

NosyParker: No . . . well, I'm sure they will when I wear them. No, there's a band here called Fusion, and they're really cool, and the singer is really cute, and I'm meeting them tonight in the diner!

CutiePie: You lie!!!

NosyParker: Au contraire, mon frère. Do a search for them – check out their website.

FashionPolice: Ella's style is très good.

NosyParker: She's really nice. I can't believe I'm gonna hang out with them! They're practically famous!

CutiePie: It's like the Mirage Mullins situation all over again!

FashionPolice: Yeah, except there's no mystery this time, is there?

NosyParker: Well, duh, yeah – how come Maff is allowed to be so cute?!!!

Mum and Nan, on the other hand, were totally unhelpful. Mum couldn't believe I wasn't going to watch her 'moment of glory', as she put it.

'Rosie, they won't know what's hit them. Little do they know that I'm in a professional Bananarama tribute act!' she said excitedly, while putting on her costume – dungarees. Don't ask.

'I'm sure you'll be great, Mum. But this band is really cool and really nice. And I haven't made any other friends here yet. *Please*, Mum?'

'Oh, OK,' she sighed. 'But are you really going to wear *that*?'

Like *she* could talk! I ignored her and turned to Nan. 'Come on, Nan, I'll walk you to number twenty-seven on my way.'

Nan had also spent the day sorting out her social life. The remote control for our TV was mysteriously 'lost' (Mum is so bad at lying!!!). However, Nan had found some people with a working TV and managed to wangle an evening with them.

'Thank you, dear,' Nan said, putting on her

raincoat, even though there wasn't a cloud in the sky. 'Come on, then. It's nearly seven!'

'Get back here by ten, Rosie!' called Mum.

'Sure thing, Mum,' I called back as Nan and I made our escape.

When I got to the American diner, I had an awful moment, standing in the doorway frantically looking for the band. I didn't recognise anyone, and the diner was pretty packed. I was sure everyone was looking at me and laughing.

I decided to go to the counter and order a drink. Then at least I could concentrate on that, and maybe see how many times I could swivel round on my swivelly stool before going back to number 42 all by myself.

'Hi . . . er, a lemonade, please,' I said to the serving person, who was wearing a bright yellow shirt. Really bright yellow. The kind of yellow Soph would team with turquoise or something. I suddenly had a wave of homesickness for the girls, and got out my phone to text them.

'Hi, Rosie!' yelled a voice right next to me.

I jumped, almost knocking over the glass that had just appeared by my hand. 'Oh, hi, Lauren,' I said.

The band was standing behind me, holding their instruments. Maff looked totally gorgeous, in a green shirt this time. Ella and Lauren had really cool make-up on, and Lauren's hair was in bunches. There was another guy with them.

'Rosie, this is Sean,' Maff said. 'He plays the guitar, too.'

'Hi, Rosie,' he said quietly – so quietly, I had to lean forwards, balancing dangerously on my stool, to hear him.

'Hi, Sean,' I said, smiling at him. And then I fell off the stool.

Luckily, Maff grabbed my elbow, so I didn't crash to my knees. Instead, I wobbled all over the place, my ankles both deciding to give way at the same time, as I shouted, 'Holy moly!' Yes, *holy moly*. How seriously uncool was that? I could hardly look at Maff. Très embarrassing!

'Are you OK, Rosie?' he asked, holding me up.

'Er, y-yes, f-fine, thanks. Sorry,' I stammered, attempting to stand up straight and act like a human being.

'Cool. Well, we need to go on stage soon, so see you later, yeah?' Maff said.

Ella smiled, linking her arm in mine. 'Come on, we've reserved you a seat.' She led me to a booth at the front of the diner, near the stage.

'Jools, this is Rosie. Rosie, this is Jools,' Lauren roared, introducing me to a bloke about Mum's age. He was wearing a suit and had a briefcase and loads of bits of paper on the table in front of him. 'He's our manager.'

'Oh – erm, hi,' I said.

'Look after her, will you, Jools?' Maff said, before winking at me and striding off with Sean to the stage.

'Sure,' said Jools, scooting over in the booth to make room for me. 'Hi, honey.'

Even though he called me 'honey', which is just really annoying, I could tell he was all right. I collapsed on the seat, grinning like an idiot, thinking, *Maff winked at me! He winked at me!*

Then I got a text:

Abs: How goes it with the hottie?

Me: Maff winked at me! ;-)

Abs: Really? He lurves you!!!

Me: Hope so. He's swoonissimo!

Abs: S here. He SO lurves you!!!

Me: Tee hee.

Abs: Me again. Hav fun 4 us!!!

Me: Got 2 go. Band playing! :-)

Fusion were awesome! They only played, like, three songs, but they had the whole diner clapping and cheering by the end. Lauren was a brilliant drummer, and Ella totally rocked the bass guitar. And Sean was good, too. But Maff – oh, Maff. He had such a great voice! Honestly, it was better than any of those reality pop star shows – you could tell he really meant what he was singing, even if it was a song about having to tidy his room. And he looked at me so often while he was singing. It was sooo cool! I totally forgot about everything, and just lost myself in the music.

When they'd finished their set, they all came back to sit with me and Jools. As they came towards the table, loads of people came up to them, including some pretty girls. They were twirling their hair *a lot* while talking to Maff. I pretended not to be watching.

'Hey, so whaddaya think?' yelled Lauren.

'You were awesome!' I said. 'Do you write the songs yourselves?'

'Yeah, Maff and I write most of them,' said Ella, 'and Lauren and Sean add in more musical bits.'

I was nodding like a mad thing to this, watching Maff laughing with a couple of girls out of the corner of my eye. 'Great! When I was backstage with Mirage Mullins once, she was humming a tune she'd just thought of –'

'You know Mirage Mullins?' gasped Ella. 'I *love* her!'

'Yeah, well, it's a long story, but me and my

mates sort of helped her out once. She's really nice.'

'Who is?' Maff asked, finally joining us.

'Mirage Mullins,' Sean said. 'Rosie is mates with her.'

'Well,' I said, 'I wouldn't say I know her *that* well. But yeah. Anyway, tell me how you guys met? Were you at school together?'

'Yeah,' yelled Lauren. 'We were all in the same class, and about two years ago we had this amazing music teacher.'

'He got us all to play current music, and was really cool. You know, so we were singing things like Coldplay instead of "Raindrops Keep Falling on My Head",' Maff said, sliding into the booth with us and taking up the story. (I was secretly glad Lauren had stopped, because there's only so long you can take being shouted at. Even in a nice way.)

'Yeah, and he encouraged us to write our own music, too,' Ella said.

'Wow, what a cool teacher! We don't have anyone like that at our school,' I said, enviously. Not that I can play an instrument, so it wouldn't be any good anyway. But how cool to have your natural talent encouraged. That teacher should have a word with Time Lord.

'Yeah, well, except he left after a year to go into the music industry himself,' Maff said.

'But by then, we were writing songs together,' Ella said. 'And we sent a demo to his record company.'

'And he pulled some strings, and we got a contract!' Lauren yelled.

Jools laughed. 'Yup. You were lucky. Most bands' demo tapes sit on someone's desk for months and months. But Gary insisted we give you a go. And we're very pleased we did!'

At this point, a yellow-shirted person appeared at our booth and took an order for burgers and more drinks. The band were on a high after their set, and when the food came, they spent ages discussing every detail of their performance. Was this bit too fast? Did Ella come in too quickly here? I just sat there, taking it all in, and sneaking quick peeks at Maff. Occasionally, he'd be looking at me too, and I'd look away and try not to go red. It was quite difficult concentrating on eating elegantly, too, especially with burgers involved – burgers whose contents squished out the other side when you tried to take a bite.

'Sorry, Rosie, this must be boring for you,' Ella said, suddenly.

'Oh, don't worry. It's all really interesting. I bet The Beatles used to have this kind of conversation the whole time.'

The band was staring at me. I started to go red. *What was I babbling about?*

But then Maff laughed, and so did the others. Phew! 'Yeah, well, we're not quite up to their standard yet, but it's nice to think they might have had the same problems!' he said.

Just then, I thought I felt my phone vibrate. I peeked at it, expecting a message from Abs or Soph, but the screen was blank – except for the time. 'Oh, no! I've got to be back in ten minutes or Mum will kill me!' I yelped.

'Are you in one of the lodges?' Maff asked.

'Yeah, number forty-two,' I said, gathering my coat and sliding out of the booth.

'I'll walk you back,' he said.

The others looked at each other.

'I, er, need to make a phone call anyway,' he said, going a bit red himself, 'and it's too loud in here.'

He was coming with me!!! 'Er, cool. Great. Right. Um . . . thanks for inviting me to watch you. You were awesome! Bye!' I said to the others.

'Bye, Rosie!' Ella and Lauren chorused.

Maff and I left the diner and, as we walked past the karaoke bar, I heard a snatch of 'Lady in Red' sung in a very warbling, very familiar voice. 'Er, so, Maff, who's your favourite celeb?' I gabbled.

He had stopped to listen. 'Wow, that singer's really going for it, isn't she?' he said, laughing.

'Yeah . . . So, favourite celebrity. Any thoughts?' I asked, grabbing his arm and dragging him outside, into the karaoke-free air. I could tell Mum was winding up the song, and I did *not* want her to bump into us.

'Well, I dunno . . .' he said. 'I don't think I have

a favourite *celebrity*, but I like a lot of bands, like The Blue Fish and Lightning.'

'Aha, you must be a Pisces then,' I said. 'Fish and weather.'

Maff laughed. 'I'm a Leo actually. But I see you are a girl of much mystic knowledge.'

'Why, yes, indeed,' I said. *Quick, think of something else to make him laugh!! Oh, too late.* Number 42 loomed ahead. 'Here we are. Chez moi.' My heart was beating really fast. A boy had walked me home!!! And a totally fit boy, too!!!

We stood there outside the door, me in the bright porch light and him in the shadows, looking all mysterious. I didn't know what to do next.

Then his phone rang. 'Hi! . . . Yeah, hang on a sec,' he said. He turned to me. 'See you tomorrow, yeah? We'll probably be at the pool at about eleven, and then have some lunch.'

'Great!' I said, far too quickly. 'Excellent. See you then.'

When I went inside, I whipped my phone out straight away to text the girls:

Me: M walked me home!

Abs: You lie!!!

Me: Au contraire. He is so gorge!

Soph: So cool!!! Lurve is in the air!

Me: Hope so!

Abs: Nite nite sleep tite don't let the love bugs bite!

Me: Ha ha. :-)

Chapter Three

The next morning, I was in a great mood. So were Mum and Nan.

'Mum, I'm going swimming and then meeting the band for lunch. Could I have some money, please?' I said, making the most of the happy moment.

'Wow, Rosie, I'm really glad you've made some friends,' Mum said 'I have as well! I met a lady called Sally last night and she loves Bananarama, too! We're going to aerobics later. Just call me if you need anything.'

Brilliant. Mum was going to be distracted by her new best friend. Things were looking up!

'I'm off to number twenty-seven again,' Nan said. 'Martha and Frank have invited me for coffee and a game of Cluedo, along with someone charming, apparently. Gerry, I believe his name is.' She giggled as she put her raincoat on.

My nan was going to meet a man! Quelle horreur! What if they fell madly in love and decided to get married? I'd probably have to be a bridesmaid and Nan would wear a big meringue dress. They'd live in another part of the country and I'd never see Nan, and Gerry's grandchildren would get all the attention. On the other hand, he might be really nice – Nan did look excited. If it made her happy, why not? I just hoped he didn't have a pointy moustache like Poirot.

After Nan had headed off to her romantic meeting, I went to mine. Well, it wasn't really a *romantic* meeting. I was just meeting the band, wasn't I? The band that happened to include the hottest boy I'd ever seen in my life!

When I got to the pool, they were all there. Maff and Sean were messing around on the diving board. Maff looked *totally* fit, even when he was pretending to fall in.

Lauren and Ella were lying by the pool. I went to sit next to them.

'Hi, Rosie!' Ella said. She was wearing an extremely cool brown kaftan, a matching headscarf and humongous sunglasses. There wasn't much point in her sunbathing – she was completely covered up.

'Hi,' I said, trying to arrange myself so I'd look my most attractive to Maff. (Legs bent or not? Lying flat, or sitting up? So many decisions! I went for one leg bent, sitting up, tummy in.)

Lauren had her MP3 player on (and a very strange hairstyle involving plaits across the top of her head), so Ella and I spent the morning chatting, watching the boys muck about in the pool. It turned out we had a lot in common. I even almost forgot to miss Abs and Soph. But then I got a text:

Soph: How R U? Hot here! No nice Fr boys.

Me: Having fun! Ella so nice. M gr8.

Soph: We miss U! Don't talk to Smella!

Me: O ha ha. Not funny. Miss U 2. U 2 still my bezzies.

Soph: Better b. x

Me: Got 2 go 4 swim now. With M!!! x

We had loads of fun splashing around in the pool. Maff kept chasing me and grabbing me. He looked so gorgeous with his hair all wet. He was wearing a really cool necklace – he said he hadn't taken it off since he got it in Mexico the year before.

After a while, my stomach started rumbling ridiculously loudly. We all went for lunch at the restaurant with the yellow chairs. I was jealous of Ella's huge sunglasses, because what with the chairs and the staff shirts, there was a *lot* of yellow in there. Maff didn't have any sunglasses – he'd broken them the week before by sitting on them, he said – and he kept trying to grab Ella's.

'Stop it!' Lauren yelled, just after Maff's arm had knocked the vinegar into her food. Being Lauren, of course her 'yell' was about a hundred times louder than anyone else's. The whole place went quiet. Everyone turned round to stare at our table. We all dissolved into giggles.

'Sorry, Lauren,' Maff said, looking sheepish and making puppy-dog eyes at her. 'Will you forgive me?'

'Only if you give me *all* your chips,' she said.

Maff sighed, melodramatically. 'Fine. Take my food. I don't need it. I'm only a growing boy.'

'Yes, and those five remaining chips will make *such* a difference,' I said.

'You'll know who to blame if I faint from hunger on stage tonight,' he replied, his hand on his forehead like he was in a costume drama or something.

Sean laughed. 'The day you faint from hunger is the day we become a Steps tribute band.'

I shuddered. Those words 'tribute band'

reminded me of Mum. 'So where did you get the name Fusion from anyway?' I asked quickly, changing the subject.

'We just liked it,' Ella said. 'It was from a physics lesson. Although Jools says it would be good if we could come up with a cool reason for it, to put on our website.'

'Oh, yeah, because at the moment there's not very much info on there, is there?' I said. Then I went bright red.

HI, I'M ROSIE. I'LL BE YOUR STALKER TODAY. COOL, AREN'T I?

Maff looked at me. 'Been checking out our website?' he asked. 'Whaddaya think of the spinning logo at the top?'

I looked blank. *What logo?*

'You know, the two blobs with lines coming out of them. It's supposed to be an atom fusing with another atom,' Sean explained.

'Oh, *that* logo,' I said. 'Yeah, it's great . . .'

'I *told* you it was rubbish,' Maff said to Sean. 'No one gets it.'

'Yeah, well, I haven't seen you come up with anything else,' Sean said.

'Guys, guys, look. We need to update the website soon anyway, so let's have a think about it, OK?' Ella said.

Suddenly, I had an idea. 'I think you should do blogs,' I blurted out.

They all looked at me.

'You know, like what you've been up to, and what you're going to do soon, so all your fans can find out the latest stuff. Everyone's doing it now. All the big names have blogs, though probably their PR people write it for them. And you're really cool, and people would love to hear about your lives, and it would get them interested in your music, so . . .' I trailed off. What *was* I going on about?

They were nodding though. 'That's a great idea, Rosie,' Maff said.

I blushed and grinned. *He thought my idea was great!!!*

'Yeah,' said Ella, getting excited. 'We could

write about how we got started, and our new album, and what we're going to do after we've played here.'

After here. I was sad for a minute. They were going to go. Well, we were all going to go. I'd just been starting to feel like part of their gang, but I wasn't. They were Fusion – a cool band – and I was just Rosie Parker, schoolgirl and part-time hanger-on to the stars.

'Hey, Rosie!' Maff said. 'How about we go check out the computer room and you show us some stuff you like. After all, you're the expert!'

OK, so he thought I was a sad fan. Still, that was nothing. Wait till he saw me log in as 'NosyParker'. That was going to be *bad* . . .

✱ ✱ ✱

'You're looking very chirpy this morning, Rosie,' Nan said when I came in to the kitchen for breakfast the next day.

'Oh, I had *such* a good day yesterday, Nan,' I said, throwing myself on to the sofa next to her.

'Fusion are so cool, and really nice, and I helped them sort out some stuff for their website. And then their gig was amazing again.'

'Oh, I'm glad you're having fun. Your mother and I were worried that you'd mope about, missing Abigail and Sophie the whole time.' Nan dived back into her Miss Marple novel while I went into a serious emotional meltdown. The girls! I hadn't texted them for ages! I pulled out my phone:

Me: Hol gr8!! How u 2?

Soph: No celebs here. :-(How's the gorge singer?

Me: He is sooo gorge!!! Look at website for photos and new blog!!

Abs: V jealous u have new celeb friends.

Me: But u 2 r best!! Have French fun!!

I love Abs and Soph, and I was sorry they weren't having as much fun as me, but I couldn't help being really pleased my holiday was turning out to be so cool!

I'd arranged to meet the band by the pool again. They had a few spare hours before Jools wanted them to rehearse. I thought they already sounded amazing, but Jools said there was no such thing as too much practice. These two weeks were sort of supposed to be Fusion's holiday, while also letting them play regular live gigs, but Jools was always working, phoning around to organise interviews – manager stuff like that. It wasn't much of a holiday for him. But I guess that's what he was paid for. It was his job to make Fusion BIG.

Maff wasn't mucking about in the pool this time when I got there. In fact, he wasn't there at all. I sat down next to Ella again. She was wearing a bikini this time, but a completely different top and bottom and a huge floppy hat.

'Hi, Rosie,' she said. 'Hey have you read this?' She tossed a magazine over to me.

'Thanks!' I settled down for some serious reading.

Lauren waved at me as she turned over on to her stomach. She had her hair in a bun this time.

What with the bright blue frames of her sunglasses, she looked a bit like a librarian. Sean had his nose deep in a music mag.

We all lay there, soaking up the sun. I couldn't believe how good the weather was. I was going to be as tanned as Soph and Abs at this rate!

After about half an hour, Maff sauntered into the pool area. My heart started to beat faster. How could I concentrate now?

'Hi,' he said, standing so his shadow covered me.

'Oi! Do you mind?' I said, laughing.

'Terribly sorry!' he said in a mock posh voice, moving to one side. 'Will the lady be requiring anything else?'

'Yes, actually,' I replied in an equally posh voice. 'I think a refreshing drink might be in order.'

'Lemonade?' he asked.

Before I could nod, Lauren sat up. 'Where have you *been*, Maff?' she screeched. 'I was looking for you. I want you to listen to something I've written.'

Maff looked uncomfortable. 'I've been around,' he said. 'Drinks, everyone?' He walked off towards the kiosk without waiting for a reply.

Ella caught my eye and shrugged. 'Boys!' she said.

Just then, Mum appeared on the other side of the pool with a woman who had to be her friend Sally. They were both wearing leotards and leggings. I quickly held the mag up to my face. Too late.

'Rosie!' Mum called. 'Coo-ee!'

I peeked over the top of the mag. What the crusty old grandads?! She was making her way over to us, jumping over sun loungers and people's towels. I slithered down my sun lounger in embarrassment.

'Rosie, there you are!' she said as she arrived next to us. 'Oh, hello, I don't think we've met. I'm Liz, Rosie's mother.' She smiled at Ella.

'Hi, I'm Ella,' Ella replied.

'So you're in this famous band then?' she asked. 'Is your manager around?'

'Er, no,' Ella said, looking confused.

'Oh,' Mum said, a bit disappointed. Sally had wandered over too, and Mum introduced me to her super-enthusiastically.

'Hi, Rosie,' Sally said chirpily. She had curly blonde hair that bounced about as she spoke.

'Yeah, hi, Sally,' I said. Oh, no! I could see Maff approaching with the drinks out of the corner of my eye. 'So, Mum, nice to see you. You should be off to your next class, right? Mustn't be late!' I trilled.

'I just wanted to say that Sally and I – and this other lovely girl we've met, Andie – are going to perform as the Banana Splits tonight in the karaoke bar at nine. You will come and watch us, won't you?'

'You're a singer too?' Maff asked.

'Oh, hello. Matt, isn't it?' she said, smiling at him. I cringed. 'Yes, we're doing a Bananarama tribute tonight. You must come and watch! And bring your manager!'

'I'd love to, but we're performing as well

tonight, I'm afraid,' Maff said.

'Yes, sorry about that, Mrs Parker,' Ella said politely.

'Oh. Well, Rosie, you'll come, won't you? Nan and Gerry are coming and it would be good if you could sit with them.' Mum looked a bit desperate.

'OK,' I said. I mean, what could I do? It seemed to mean a lot to her. Maybe I could get out of it later?

'Great!' She beamed and kissed my cheek. 'Right, come on, Sally! We need to practise our moves!'

They marched off, and I groaned.

'She seems really nice,' Ella said.

'Yeah, well, she is, I suppose. But she's so embarrassing! I mean, *Bananarama* for goodness sake!' I said.

'Yes, Rosie, who *are* Bananarama?' Maff asked.

'An eighties girl band originally comprising Keren, Sara and Siobhan, who had hits such as "Robert De Niro's Waiting" and "I Want You Back",' said Sean without looking up.

We all stared at him.

'What?' he said. 'This magazine is very informative, you know.'

Ella started giggling and then we were all laughing. Maff punched Sean on the arm. What a miracle! They'd met my mother and they still wanted to hang around with me.

* * *

A bit later, after we'd played tag in the pool, Maff came up to my sun lounger.

'Do you want to grab some lunch?' he asked.

I looked at Ella. 'I'm not hungry,' she said.

'Sure, that would be nice,' I said, putting my shorts and flip-flops on. I sounded calmer than I felt. This was practically a date – just me and him, on our own, eating. Well, if I was able to eat anything. My stomach was in knots.

Even though I was really tense, lunch actually went well. Maff was so nice, asking questions about my life and being really funny. He was very impressed by my Mirage Mullins story, and he said he'd like to meet Abs and Soph one day. And who wouldn't? If I do say so myself, my friends are p-r-e-t-t-y cool.

After lunch, we went for a walk outside the holiday park, along the cliff path that leads to town. The guard at the gate nodded at Maff as if he knew him. I suppose you get used to that when you're almost famous.

The sun was shining and we had a full ten minutes before Maff had to be back rehearsing with the band. The only thing missing was an ice cream – that would have been perfect.

'So, what do your parents think about the band?' I asked Maff. 'They must be sooo proud of you.'

He bent down and picked a flower. 'Yeah . . . well, they were a bit worried about me leaving school at sixteen, but I convinced them this is what I want to do. I've been thinking about them a lot recently actually . . .' Maff stared into the distance for a bit before shaking himself. 'Anyway, how can they say I'm not hitting the big time? I mean, we're playing Smallhampton Holiday Park!'

I laughed. 'My mum thinks this is the best place ever. They have to drag her off stage every night!'

Maff smiled. 'She's really keen, isn't she? I bet she's good.'

I looked at him. Maff was so lovely. And so utterly wrong. 'In a recent poll, eight out of ten dogs said they'd like to howl along with her.'

Maff laughed. 'You're so mean!!! We can't all be talented.'

He waggled his eyebrows at me and I hit him on the arm. 'Or modest,' I said.

'Hey, I've got to get back,' Maff said, looking at his watch. 'Time for rehearsal.'

As we turned round our hands accidentally brushed together. He looked at the flower he was holding.

'Here,' he said, handing it to me.

HE LIKES ME! HE LIKES ME!

✳ ✳ ✳

Even though I really tried, I couldn't get out of going to see Mum perform. I was gutted to miss the Fusion gig, but at least it meant they couldn't watch Mum – although Maff had threatened to cancel their performance and come along.

The best bit of the evening was meeting Nan's new 'friend' Gerry. He looked a bit like Jack Frost from *A Touch of Frost* actually, if you squinted – moustache and all.

'A pleasure to meet you, Rosie,' he said, kissing my hand. 'I've heard so much about you.'

I looked at Nan suspiciously. She blinked innocently. 'Gerry's a retired colonel, you know,' she said. 'Won lots of medals.'

'Oh?' I said, not really knowing what to say. *For what? Which war?*

'Yes, well, let's not get into that,' Gerry said, sticking out his chest with pride. 'Now, let me get you two ladies a drink.'

The less said about the Banana Splits the better, although I have to say Sally is a good singer. Better than Mum, actually. Not that I told *her* that. I was in her good books and if I wanted to hang around with Fusion for the next week or so, I had to stay there. And I totally meant to hang around with Fusion for as long as they would put up with me. This holiday was turning out to be the best one *ever*!!!

Chapter Four

Over the next few days, I hardly saw Mum and Nan, I was so busy with Fusion. They were both very busy anyway. Nan and Gerry had really hit it off, and she spent most of her time playing bingo or watching TV with him and her friends at number 27. Meanwhile, Mum and Sally attended all the aerobics classes and karaoke nights there were. And there were a *lot*. Mum kept trying to get me to introduce her to Jools ('I'm sure he'd love to hear us sing, Rosie . . .'), but I'd managed to avoid it so far.

And me? Well, in between hanging out with the band at the pool, having lunch with them, and watching them play in the evenings, there was very little time to do other vital things – paint my toenails, eat ice creams, try on all my clothes a hundred times, try to look a little bit cooler (Ella and Lauren set high standards of coolness). Most important of all, I had to keep up with the goss!

NosyParker: Bonjour, mes amis.

CutiePie: So, how come you're not with Smella?

NosyParker: Don't call her that!! Ella and the others are rehearsing. But check this: Maff wants to put a picture of me on their website!!! As part of the crowd at their gig. But still!!!

FashionPolice: Ooooh!! It must be lurve!!

NosyParker: I wish you girls could meet him. He's so gorgey, and so funny. . .

CutiePie: And famous! You are so lucky, Rosie Parker!!!

NosyParker: I know!!! In your face, Amanda Hawkins!!!

The band was doing really well – their gigs were getting so popular the holiday park had decided to open them to people who weren't staying there. So the diner was really crowded now – with pretty girls, mostly. The band was getting loads of hits on their website as well, and they asked me to help think of things to put on their blog each day.

'I think we should host a barbecue for the holiday park, to say thank you,' Jools said, halfway through the fortnight. 'We'll have it on the beach and invite local press and radio. It'll be great PR. What do you reckon?'

Everyone agreed it was a great idea. Well, everyone except Maff, who was late again. He had been turning up late a lot recently and it really annoyed the others. Especially Jools, who'd work hard to organise an interview or something and then Maff wouldn't be there. He would never say where he'd been either – 'Oh, just around . . .' –

and he never answered his phone.

In his absence, I compiled the following list in my head:

Top ten reasons why I like Maff!!!:

1. He's hot!
2. He's really talented at singing and playing the guitar and writing songs.
3. He's really funny.
4. He's got gorgey blue eyes.
5. He's really cool. He's got stage presence in bucket-loads when he's up there singing. Mr Lord would love him. 'Presence. That's what you need to be a great actor, Rosie,' he always says. 'Not the ability to giggle and cavort about with your friends.'
6. He's really nice. And he listens when you tell him stuff.
7. He said he wanted to meet my best friends, so he might want to see me again!!!!!
8. He likes my frog wellies!!

9. He's mysterious – always going off by himself without telling anyone where he's going. I reckon that's when he's thinking about new songs.

10. He's GORGEOUS!!!!!!!!!!!!!!!!!

Anyway, when he finally turned up, Maff agreed a barbecue was a great idea. It was supposed to be just for holiday-park staff and press – no fans – but he asked Jools if I could come too.

'Rosie's been really helpful with the website,' he said.

'Yeah – she's practically writing the blog for us,' Ella said.

'OK, fine,' Jools said. 'But no one else.'

Maff grinned at me and I grinned back. He was sooo nice!!!

✳ ✳ ✳

The girls agreed I HAD to look totally hot at the barbecue. I tried to wangle some money for a new outfit out of Mum, but she wasn't having any of it.

'You've brought almost your entire wardrobe with you, Rosie,' she said. 'I'm sure you can find *something* to wear. You can borrow something of mine if you like.'

I shuddered. No *way* would I wear anything of Mum's!!! I went back to my room to look at my clothes again.

Eventually, I confessed to Ella that I had nothing to wear.

'Hey, you can wear one of my dresses, Rosie,' she said.

'Really? Great!' I was thrilled, but also wary. I'd had enough makeover experiences with Soph before to know that other people's style doesn't necessarily work on me.

The day of the barbecue, I went round to Ella and Lauren's lodge. Lauren was bouncing up and down on her bed, her loose hair flying everywhere, wearing skinny jeans and a vest top. So simple, yet so cool. Ella had a yellow-and-pink dress on, with a green T-shirt underneath. I knew I'd look really stupid in something like that – I was praying she'd have something more normal for me.

And she did! By the time she'd finished, I was wearing a blue skirt that exactly matched my eyes (apparently) and a funky pale yellow T-shirt, and Lauren had put my hair into a chignon (also known as a bun). I actually felt quite elegant. Especially when Ella made me wear my sandals rather than my trainers.

I couldn't believe it when I looked in the mirror. I looked totally different. Maff would be bowled over when he saw me. He might ask me to dance. Maybe he'd even kiss me!!! We'd start going out and I'd follow Fusion all over the world, helping Jools do the band's PR (as I was clearly a PR genius). Maff would never look at any of the band's groupies; he'd only have eyes for me . . .

'Ready?' Ella asked, breaking in on my daydream. 'You look great, Rosie. Maff's totally going to fancy you!'

I blushed. She'd guessed I fancied him! How embarrassing!

The barbecue was fantastic. They had put

loads of candles in glasses on the path through the dunes to the beach. Even though it wasn't dark yet, the flickering flames looked amazing. Jools was in charge of the barbecue, waving his tongs around while he was talking. Everyone was standing around drinking punch.

Obviously, the band members were supposed to be talking to the press. 'It's all about the PR, darling,' Lauren had yelled at me earlier – as she plaited her hair into a French braid with a pink ribbon threaded through it – so I knew they wouldn't have much time to talk to me.

But as soon as we arrived, Maff came up to us. 'Wow. You look . . . great, Rosie,' he said softly. I blushed. 'Thanks! You look nice, too.' NICE? HE LOOKED TOTALLY HOT!!!

At this point, Jools called Maff over to meet someone, but he smiled at me before he went. I decided to hover by the food table and just people-watch. Well, OK, Maff-watch.

After about ten minutes of talking to the journalist, Maff got Sean involved, then looked around for me. Our eyes met, and I started fiddling nervously with the tablecloth as he wove through the crowd, heading for me. But before he got close, he was cornered by one of the holiday-park bar staff, still in her bright yellow shirt.

Jools was starting to pass out the food now, so I got myself a burger and went to the salad table – which just happened to be very close to where Maff and this girl were standing.

While he was talking to the girl and I was on the other side of the table, getting some ketchup for my burger, he looked at me with his big blue eyes and I *swear* my heart did a flip. I was so surprised I forgot I was pouring ketchup, so I got a lot more than I really needed on my quarter pounder. But hey, I like ketchup. Not as much as I like Maff though!!!

Once he'd got rid of the girl, he came over to me. 'Hey, you,' he said softly.

'Mmmph,' I said, trying to swallow the mouthful I'd just taken. Bad timing or what?

'I've got something to show you,' he said. 'Come over here.'

I followed him to a row of fairy lights strung between poles in the sand. We sat down on two deckchairs underneath them.

'I haven't shown the others this yet,' he said, getting a piece of paper out of his shirt pocket. 'It's the beginnings of a new song. I wanted to see what you thought first.' He passed the paper to me.

Oh! He was showing me first. I couldn't believe it. What if I said something stupid?

The song was called 'One Week', and this is how it went:

One week since I saw you,
One week since I met you.
I have so much I want to say,
I need to see you every day.

You make everything real,
I want to tell you how I feel.
It's only one week since I saw you,
One week since I met you.

Soon we'll have to part,
But you'll stay in my heart.
One week since I met you,
A lifetime to remember you.

As I read it, I realised Maff was humming quietly next to me.

'This is the tune,' he said, starting to hum again.

I listened to him, reading the words over and over. Unless I was totally wrong, the words were about me!!! Weren't they? They had to be! I'd first met him a week ago, after all.

'So, what do you think?' he asked me, looking into my eyes.

I gulped. My heart was hammering. 'I think it's beautiful,' I said. 'Really amazing.'

He grinned and was about to say something when Lauren bounded over. 'Maff! Time for photos!' she yelled.

Maff smiled apologetically at me and stood up. He took the lyrics from me and put his finger to his lips.

I nodded and watched them go over to where a photographer was trying to get a shot of them with the sunset in the background. How fab was that?? I was the first person to see Fusion's new song – and it was about *me*!!! I had to tell the girls:

Me: M has written song about me!!!
Abs: You lie!!!
Me: All true, I swear.
Abs: Sooo cool!!

Now all I had to do was work out how to get the next few days to last forever.

Chapter Five

The next morning I went to the pool to meet the band as usual, but Maff wasn't there.

'Hi, Rosie,' Ella said. She looked a bit worried. 'You haven't seen Maff, have you?'

'Not since last night,' I said.

'Oh, dear.'

'Why, what's wrong?'

'Well, no one's seen him all morning . . .' Ella began.

'And his bed hasn't been slept in!' yelled Lauren, flinging her hair over her shoulder.

'Oh,' I said. 'Well, he often disappears, doesn't he? Maybe he wanted to be alone this morning.'

'Yeah, but where was he last night?' Ella said. 'He's not answering his mobile and we've searched everywhere in the holiday park. It's really weird.'

I was worried now. They were all looking at me as though I should know what to do. Where was Abs when I needed her? France, that's where. If only I hadn't told them about helping Mirage Mullins, they wouldn't expect me to sort it out. I had to pull myself together.

'OK, well, let's search again. And keep trying his mobile. Why don't we meet back here in an hour? I'll check the games rooms.'

'Good idea,' said Sean. 'I'll check the sports courts. Jools is down on the beach now.'

'We'll look in the restaurants then,' said Ella. 'See you later.'

We all walked off in different directions.

Maff had a habit of disappearing, it was true. But why hadn't his bed been slept in? I had this awful feeling in the pit of my stomach. After all, now Fusion was getting more and more well known, he could be a target for someone crazy. Practically every celebrity had a stalker these days. *No, you're letting your imagination get to you, Rosie! He's just gone for a long walk or something.*

After I'd checked the games rooms – and waved at Nan and Gerry, who were playing bingo – I went to the computer room in case Maff was there, updating the blog. But he wasn't. I still had loads of time before meeting the others and I really needed to tell the girls what was happening. I texted Soph to tell her to get to a computer – like, now! Then I logged on.

NosyParker: Maff's gone missing!!!

CutiePie: Are you sure?

NosyParker: His bed wasn't slept in.

FashionPolice: Oh. That's bad. Have you searched everywhere?

NosyParker: Yes, but we can't find him.

FashionPolice: Maybe he's been kidnapped by some crazy girl fans?!?!

NosyParker: Not funny. Seriously, I'm worried.

CutiePie: Look, there must be an explanation. He's probably writing another song about you somewhere!!

NosyParker: Well, he does go off by himself sometimes.

FashionPolice: Why?????

NosyParker: Dunno. He goes all secretive when we ask him.

CutiePie: Talk to Smella and the band. They know him best.

NosyParker: Yeah, good plan, Stan. AND DON'T CALL HER THAT!

When I met up with the others, they'd had no luck either. And Jools was back from the beach, shaking his head.

'Honestly, what *does* he think he's playing at?' Jools said, exasperated. 'He normally only skips off for an hour or so, but he's been ages. Why isn't he answering his phone?'

'I'm sure he would if it was working,' Ella said, sitting on a sun lounger in despair. 'The battery's probably run out. He always forgets to charge it.'

'I'm sorry. I know he's not stupid,' Jools said. 'Just annoying, the way he keeps disappearing! I'm getting worried though. I'm supposed to be responsible for you guys, and now he's missing.'

'I'm sure he'll turn up soon,' I said hopefully. 'Are you positive he didn't come home last night, Sean?'

'Yeah. I mean, I was pretty tired, so I left the barbecue after the reporters had gone, but I didn't hear him come into the bedroom, and he's normally really noisy. His usual thing is to start playing some new tune that's in his head last thing at night. But I slept through last night and his bed is still made. Maff never makes his bed.'

'Look, we're booked to do that phone interview for the local radio station now,' said Jools. 'We're going to have to do it without him. We'll say he's ill. Rosie, could you keep searching? We'll see you back here after the interview – maybe he'll have turned up.'

'Yeah, sure,' I said, glad to be of some use.

The band hugged me and left, following Jools. I sighed. Where on earth could he be? I decided to wander around again.

By the time I meandered back into the games rooms, my mind was working overtime. Half of me was convinced Maff was going to saunter in at any minute with that big smile on his face. The other half was imagining finding his dead body somewhere. That was Nan's influence – you can't watch nine billion detective shows without being convinced there are murderers everywhere. Speaking of whom . . .

'Hello, Rosie,' Nan said. She'd just finished another exciting game of bingo. 'Why are you looking down in the dumps? Lost your boyfriend?'

'He's not my boyfriend,' I said automatically, going red. 'Anyway, I have lost him, yes.'

'Well, I'm afraid men can be a bit fickle, love,' Nan said sympathetically. She patted my arm.

'No, I don't mean like *that*. He's gone missing!' I cried.

'Oh, dear. Sit down, love.' Nan sat down at an empty bingo table, and patted the seat next to her. 'When did you last see him?' she asked, her head on one side.

'Last night, at the barbecue,' I said, sitting down too.

'Hmmm. This reminds me of an episode of *Miss Marple* –' she began.

I interrupted her before she could get into the details. 'Apparently he didn't sleep in his bed last night!'

'Really? Well, that *is* worrying.'

Now Gerry joined us. 'Ah, Rosie,' he said. 'Have you come to play bingo with your enchanting grandmother?'

Nan looked rather pleased at being called 'enchanting', but tried to hide it. 'We've got a problem here, Gerry,' she said. 'The singer from that band has disappeared. Matt.'

'Maff,' I muttered despairingly.

'Yes, Maff. He hasn't been seen for a while and he didn't sleep in his bed last night.'

'Have you tried calling his mobile telephone? You young people are surgically attached to your phones, aren't you?' Gerry said, winking at me.

I sighed. Like I wouldn't have thought of that. 'It's going straight to his voicemail.'

'Rosie, didn't you say that he often disappears?' Nan asked.

'Yeah, but I don't know where to.'

'Well, I bet I know someone who does. Follow me.' Nan got up. 'My coat, Gerry.'

Gerry held out her raincoat for her and then took her arm. They moved towards the exit, ignoring the bingo caller's cries for everyone to take their seats for the next game.

Shrugging, I followed them. In the absence of Abs and Soph, they were the best back-up I had.

I was totally confused when we ended up at reception. What was Nan doing?

'Could you tell me if Judy is working today, please?' she asked the yellow-shirted receptionist.

'Yes, she's currently doing lodges thirty-one to forty,' the woman replied, looking a bit bemused.

'Thank you – I just wanted to ask her something,' Nan called as she headed to the door.

So off we went to lodges 31 to 40. Very slowly. Gerry, it became clear, couldn't walk very fast. He and Nan were leaning against each other, which made our progress very slow. But I was happy to keep to their pace. *Not*.

'Nan, what are we doing?' I asked. 'Who is this Judy person?'

'All will become clear soon enough,' she replied, mysteriously. Honestly, it was like she thought we were in one of her detective shows.

'Nan!!!' I said.

'Oh, OK, Judy's the cleaner here, and she knows things. You'll see.'

I had to admit it was a good idea. Staff members always see things other people miss. I too have learnt this from Jessica Fletcher. Hopefully Judy could shed some light on this mystery, because I was at a loss. All I wanted was to see Maff again.

When we found Judy, she was scrubbing the bathroom of number 36.

'Hello, Pam,' she cried. 'You were right – this Mr Shiny stuff really works!'

'Oh, good,' Nan said. 'I do think it gives bathrooms that extra gleam.'

'Nan!!!' I said. *Maff's missing and she's talking about cleaning products!*

'Oh, yes, sorry, Rosie. Judy, this is my granddaughter Rosie.'

'You're the one who's always with that band, aren't you?' Judy said.

I didn't have time to be amazed that she'd noticed. 'Yes!' I said. 'D'you know Maff? The tall one with blue eyes?'

'Ooh, yes,' Judy said cheerfully.

'He's gone missing!'

'We wanted to ask you if you'd seen him at all,' Nan said, sitting down on the bed. Gerry sat down next to her. I think he was a bit out of puff.

'Well, let me think. I've seen him a few times lately. You lot are always out and about, aren't you?' Judy said. 'Now, I saw him at the park gates yesterday, I think. Yes, yesterday. Talking to a man.'

'Really?' I said, perking up. *This could be a clue!* 'What time was it?'

'Well, I'd just come off my lunch break, so it must have been about two o'clock.'

'Oh.' That was before we went to the beach for a swim. I remembered now that we'd had to wait for Maff to turn up before we set off. I'd just thought he was late as usual.

'So, what did this man look like?' Nan asked.

'Well, he's sort of medium height, brown hair, wears jeans . . .' Judy said, pulling the pink rubber gloves off her hands.

Great, I thought. *That's only like every single man in Smallhampton then.* 'Have you seen him more than once?' I asked.

'Ooh, yes. I've seen him talking to Maff several times,' Judy said, nodding.

'Really? Thanks, Judy! Thanks, Nan!' I kissed her on the cheek and legged it to tell the band.

Only Ella was at the pool, slumped on a sun lounger.

'Ella!' I shouted. 'I might have a lead!' I skidded

to a stop next to her, just managing not to fall in the pool. 'Judy, who cleans the chalets, reckons she's seen Maff talking to some bloke at the park gates. She saw him there yesterday before we went to the beach, and a few other times, too.'

'Who could that be?' Ella wondered.

Just then, I got a text. I whipped my phone out, hoping it was Maff, but it was the girls.

> **Soph:** Found him yet?
> **Me:** No!! But he met a bloke yesterday. And the day before.
> **Soph:** Who???
> **Me:** Dunno.
> **Soph:** Sounds dodgy. What's happening?
> **Me:** Dunno!! What next?
> **Soph:** Find bloke, then u find Maff.

'We've got to find this man,' I said.

Ella nodded. 'I'll come with you. The others are searching the town and the beach again. Jools says if we haven't found him by two o'clock, he's calling the police.'

I gulped. This was getting serious. It was twelve o'clock now. But we had some hope. If only we could get Judy to describe the man in more detail, we might be getting somewhere. We rushed back to lodge 36.

Judy wasn't there.

'Oh, no!' I wailed. *Don't panic, Rosie* . . .

'Let's try the next lodge along,' Ella said.

We eventually found Judy in number 39. 'Hello again,' she said.

'This is Ella, she's in the band,' I said. 'Can you describe the man you saw with Maff again?'

'Well, I'm not very good at describing . . .' Judy began.

'How many times did you see him?' asked Ella.

'Ooh, let me see . . . About four or five times, I guess. They were often chatting at the gates.'

'So that's why he was always late,' Ella said. 'But I wonder who this man is. Oh – I hope he's not a rival record producer!'

'I'm sure he isn't! But he could be anyone.' I gasped as a thought struck me. 'He could have kidnapped Maff! Judy, do you think you'd recognise him again?'

'Well, maybe . . .' Judy said.

'Great! He's probably staying in the town. Will you help us look for him?'

'Ooh, I don't know . . . I'm not supposed to leave the park on a shift.'

'Please? It's really important we find Maff!' I pleaded. 'I'll help you clean the toilets for the rest of my stay if you do!' A tiny part of my mind said, 'Ew!', but I ignored it. This was an emergency.

Judy laughed. 'You take after your grand-mother – can't wait to use Mr Shiny. OK, go on then. I'll come into town for a bit. But you'll have to wait. I've got to finish these lodges first.'

Ella and I looked at each other. 'We'll help!'

When we found Maff, he would *seriously* owe us one.

Chapter Six

An hour and a broken nail later, we were sitting in the café on the main high street of Smallhampton, hoping this mysterious man would walk past. OK, so it wasn't a brilliant plan, but we didn't have any other option. Well, we could have knocked on every door in Smallhampton and asked, 'Are you the man who was talking to Maff at the holiday park this week?' That was *so* not going to work.

We'd positioned Judy so she had a good view, and she was enjoying her cup of tea a lot. 'Ooh, it's nice to have a bit of a sit-down. And thank you for your help. Those bathrooms were really gleaming by the time we'd finished, weren't they?'

'Er, yes,' Ella replied, picking the label off her bottle of juice.

I bit my ragged nail in frustration. We'd been there for ages and not one man had walked past. How strange was that? It was like my mum always says: when you want a man, there's none to be had.

Ella sighed. She was clearly thinking the same thing as me: just ten minutes more, then we'd start walking round town by ourselves, because Judy had to go back to work. But we didn't know who to look for. Anyway, Sean and Jools had already searched the town for Maff and had no luck. Aaargh – it was hopeless!

Suddenly, Judy sat up straight. Then she slumped again. 'No, not him,' she said. 'Or him.'

Finally some blokes were appearing. I turned round to see a sudden flood of men in the street. Odd. Where had they been before? I glanced over the road and saw a pub with a blackboard listing football games. There had been a game on – England against Portugal. I remembered Maff and Sean talking about it, going on about how it was time for revenge after Portugal had beaten us in the 2006 World Cup. I couldn't believe Maff would have missed the game!

'Judy, keep your eyes peeled!' I said.

'I am, dear. This is exciting, isn't it? Now, he had a sort of dark green coat on, I think . . .'

'Like that one?' Ella said, pointing at a bloke who was coming out of the pub.

'Yes! That's him!' Judy said.

'Really?' I said, leaping up from my chair. 'Are you sure?'

'Yes, pretty sure,' Judy said. It would have to do. Ella and I ran out of the café. The man had walked up the road into a newsagent's. We followed him in and hovered by the crisps. He looked pretty normal: brown hair, green coat, jeans. He was probably about my mum's age. In fact, she'd definitely like him if she met him.

Stop it, Rosie! He's probably got Maff tied up in some

room somewhere, and you're thinking about whether your mum would fancy him! Get a grip!

There was a bit of a queue in the shop – it took him ages to buy his paper. We were waiting by the crisps for so long I got quite peckish.

'I might get some salt and vinegar,' I whispered to Ella, who was peering round the shelves at the man.

'OK. I like cheese and onion. And I like the look of those milkshakes, too,' she whispered back.

'So what are we going to do when he leaves the shop?' I asked, piling crisps and bottles of milkshake into my arms.

'Follow him!' Ella said, her eyes gleaming. 'We've got to find out if he's got Maff hidden somewhere!'

I gulped. What were we going to do if he did? We should have got Sean to come along, too, in case things got nasty. But it was too late now – the man was leaving!

I ran up and fumbled in my pocket for money. The bloke at the till took ages to find change for the man in front of me. I just hoped that Ella had kept the mystery man firmly in her sights. We couldn't let him get away!!!

Finally, I handed over my money and ran out of the shop after Ella. I caught up with her at the end of the road. We sauntered casually behind the man, pretending we weren't following him. We paused to look in shop windows every now and then, so we didn't get too close. I saw some nice stuff, actually. If we hadn't been following him, I could have bought a really great bikini!

The man went down a street, and let himself into a house. Ella and I positioned ourselves on the wall opposite, watching and waiting. And eating.

'So what's the story, Rory?' I asked.

'Dunno. Maybe wait until he goes out again, and then sneak over and look in any windows we can reach to see if he's got Maff in there,' Ella replied. Her phone beeped. 'Still no sign of him, Sean says. Jools is seriously scared now.'

She looked at me. 'Shall I tell them what we're doing?'

I thought about it. 'No, they'll think we're crazy. Just say we're looking for Maff in town and will be back soon.'

'We won't be able to play our gig tonight without him,' Ella said sadly. 'I can't believe he's not here, hanging about and making silly jokes.'

'I know. I really miss him,' I said quietly.

We sat there in silence for a bit. Well, silent apart from crisp-crunching sounds anyway. Then, suddenly –

'He's leaving!' Ella hissed, nudging me. I nearly choked on a crisp.

'OK, act cool. We're just hanging out, remember?' I said.

The man glanced at us as he left, but we both gazed down at Ella's phone as if it was the most fascinating thing ever. He soon disappeared round the corner.

'Quick!' said Ella.

We ran across the road and into the front garden. Ella peered into the windows either side of the front door. 'No, nothing.'

'Hey, there's a gate here,' I said, pushing it. 'It's open. Shall we go round the back?'

Ella paused. Then, 'Yeah!' she said. 'We've got to save Maff!'

We snuck round the side of the house and found ourselves in the back garden. We could see into the kitchen from there, and it was empty.

Oh, no. What are we going to do now? 'Well, I guess that's the end of *that* lead,' I said.

Ella nodded, looking miserable. 'I was so sure he was going to be here.'

I looked through the kitchen window again, and saw a copy of the Fusion poster from the holiday park lying on the table. I gasped. 'Look, Ella! He's got one of your posters! He knows who you are! Maybe he's been stalking you! Maff could be inside right now, tied up and unable to call for help!'

Ella looked at me. I could tell she was wavering.

I thought quickly. What would Abs and Sophie say? I knew the answer. *Rescue him!!!* 'Come on,' I said. 'Let's see if there's an open window or something we could squeeze through.'

'But we can't just go into a stranger's house!!' Ella said, shocked.

'I know. We shouldn't,' I said. 'But Maff could be in there!!'

There was a short pause. I thought of all the reasons why we shouldn't do it.

Top five reasons never to break into a stranger's house:

1. It's illegal!!!
2. What would we say if we got caught?
3. There could be an accomplice in the house!!!
4. My mum would kill me! And my nan would too.
5. We weren't equipped for breaking in – no gloves. We could leave fingerprints!!

But . . .

'Well, we're here now . . .' Ella said.

'Yes! Come on, let's have a really quick look

and then we'll go. He'll never know we were here.'

'What if he has a burglar alarm?' Ella whispered.

'Then we run! Anyway, the alarm won't work if there's already a window open,' I said, sounding more positive than I felt. 'I just know this man has got something to do with Maff's disappearance!'

'OK, OK,' Ella said. She was standing by the back door. 'Well, I may as well try this.' She bent down and lifted up the back door mat, uncovering a key. 'He's not very security conscious, is he?!' she whispered, unlocking the door and opening it.

'Thank goodness!' I replied.

We crept in, waiting for an alarm to go off, but there was just silence. It was really eerie, actually. I couldn't help shivering with excitement and fear. Well, mostly fear, to be honest. What if the man came back? What if Maff wasn't here? But I was sure we'd find a clue at least.

We stuck our heads round the lounge door, but there was no Maff. He wasn't in the dining room either.

'Quick! Let's check upstairs,' Ella said. 'Before the man comes back.'

We were just creeping up the stairs when we heard a key in the lock. The man was back – and there was nowhere to run!!!

Chapter Seven

He spotted us as soon as he opened the door. 'Who are you? What are you doing in my house?' he shouted.

We were frozen to the spot, unable to speak. Ella clutched my arm.

'Come on! What are you doing? Answer me or I'm calling the police!' He got his phone out of his pocket, not taking his eyes off us for a minute.

'No, don't! We're, er, we're friends of Maff's,' I stammered. *Duh, why did I mention him? Now he'll probably kidnap us too!!!*

'Maff?' the man said, pausing.

'Yes, Matthew Tucker. He's in a band with me,' Ella said.

'Ah, yes, Fusion,' the man said.

'Yeah, and we know you've been talking to him this week at the holiday park,' I said bravely. This was pretty scary. I wished we'd told Sean where we were when we replied to his text.

'Oh, you do, do you?' the man said. He put his phone down on the hall table and smiled suddenly – a big wide smile like Maff's. 'Come down then, you two. You don't have to be afraid.'

Ella and I looked at each other. What was going on? And where was Maff? 'People know where we are,' I lied.

'Look, you've got nothing to worry about. I won't call the police. If you're friends of Maff's, you're friends of mine. Come on, let's have a chat.' He gestured towards the lounge.

We slowly came down the stairs. We both had our hands on our mobiles, in case he suddenly did something.

'Look, I'll put the kettle on and we can talk properly,' the man called, going into the kitchen.

Ella and I went into the lounge and sat down on the sofa, very close together.

'What do you think his plan is?' whispered Ella.

'I don't know – we should be ready to run at any moment. But he might be all right. Let's hear what he has to say,' I said. I was petrified, but I didn't want to show it.

Ella slipped her arm through mine for security.

The man came in and sat down opposite us. 'The kettle's on,' he said. 'Right, I'm Steve. And you are?'

'Ella,' Ella said nervously.

Should we have given false names? Oh, well, too late now, I thought. 'I'm Rosie,' I said.

'Oh, yes, Maff's talked about you both,' Steve said.

'Has he?' I said.

'Yes, he loves writing songs with you, Ella. He says you're very talented. And he told me he was pleased he'd met you, Rosie.' Steve winked at me.

I blushed. Well, if Maff had told him stuff like that he *must* be all right. But why would Maff talk to him about us?

'How do you know Maff anyway?' I asked casually.

The man paused. 'Ah, well. Now that's an interesting question.' He got up. 'Tea?'

We both nodded and he left the room again.

'This is so weird,' Ella whispered. 'It seems he's Maff's friend.'

'But why were they meeting in secret at the gates?' I wondered. 'There's definitely something odd going on.'

Steve came back in with three mugs of tea. Ella and I had to disentangle our arms to hold our mugs, but I kept my other hand on my mobile in my pocket, just in case.

'So, are you a relative of Maff's?' Ella asked him.

Steve laughed. 'Well, you could say that . . . No point in beating around the bush. I'm his dad.'

Ella and I looked at each other, totally bemused.

'But I've met his dad back home,' said Ella. 'You're not him.'

'No, I'm his *birth* dad. Maff's adopted.'

'Ohhhhhh,' I said. 'Wow.'

'Yeah, wow,' he said. 'Maff got in contact with me about six months ago and we've been writing to each other ever since. When he told me he and the band had been booked to play at the holiday park, I decided to rent a place down here so we could meet up, away from his adoptive parents. He hasn't told them about me yet.'

'Wow,' Ella said. 'I didn't know.'

'Well, we haven't really spent that much time together. I think Maff wanted to keep it a secret until he got to know me. Just to check his dad wasn't totally embarrassing!' He laughed. 'Anyway, now it's your turn. Why were you sneaking around here?'

'Maff's gone missing,' I explained. 'We, er . . . well . . . when we heard about you meeting him, we didn't know who you were and we thought you might have kidnapped him.' I blushed. It sounded so ridiculous now.

'What do you mean, he's missing?' Steve said, putting his tea down on the table and staring at me.

'We haven't seen him all day, and his bed wasn't slept in last night,' Ella explained. 'You were our only lead. But if you've seen him . . .'

Steve had gone white. 'I haven't seen him since last night. He phoned from a party on the beach and asked if he could come over to talk. We had a good long chat and he said he was going for a walk to think about everything. He needed to work out how to break the news to his adoptive parents – that he'd met me, I mean. He was going back to the park!'

'Well, he didn't get there!' I said. I was getting seriously stressed again.

'Oh, no, this is all my fault! I knew I should have dropped him at the gates,' Steve moaned, his head in his hands.

'Did he say where he was going?' Ella asked him, urgently.

'He muttered something about walking the long

way back to the holiday park, to clear his head . . .'

Ella and I looked at each other in horror. What if he'd taken the cliff path? It was really dangerous in the dark.

Oh, no! I thought. I leapt up. 'He must be still up there! He could be hurt! I'm going to find him!'

'Don't go by yourself, Rosie!' Steve said as I ran out of the room. 'Wait! I'm calling the police now! They'll find him!'

But I was on a mission. I couldn't bear the thought of Maff lying there. Why hadn't I thought of the cliff path before? Stupid, stupid Rosie! If he'd been there all night . . . well, I just hoped I'd find him soon.

I ran up the road to the footpath that lead on to the cliffs. It was one of the routes back to the holiday park, and it made sense that Maff would have returned that way from Steve's if he'd wanted to clear his head.

'Maff!' I shouted. 'Maff!!! Where are you?' I could have done with Lauren to help me, with her booming voice. 'Maff!!!'

I soon got a stitch from running so fast and I had to slow to a walk. But I still called and called.

It wasn't a nice summer's day any more – it was as if the weather knew how desperate I was and had changed to suit my mood. The wind was battering my face, blowing my hair into my eyes. Clouds were gathering on the horizon. There was no one about. All I could see was grass and more grass on my right and the cliff edge on my left. No Maff. No anything. Not even anyone walking their dog.

'Maff! Where are you?' I called in despair. I couldn't believe it. I was so sure he'd be here. I stopped walking. This was pointless. What was I going to do? Where *was* he?

I went to the edge of the cliff and looked across at the horizon. The light coming through the clouds was bright and sparkled on the sea. The wind was still blowing my hair into my face. All I could think of was Maff, alone somewhere and unable to call for help. I was exhausted and worried and in despair. I burst into tears and sank to my knees, sobbing. I couldn't believe that I'd thought I'd found a lead, but I still didn't know where Maff was.

I peered carefully over the edge, thinking how high the cliff was. Then I saw something dark down below, on a ledge just a little way down the cliff.

It moved, and my heart leapt. 'Maff!!!' I yelled. There was more movement below – a hand waving!

There he was! And he was still alive!!!

Chapter Eight

I knew what to do immediately. I got my phone and dialled the emergency number.

'Hello . . . Ambulance please . . . I'm on the cliffs just outside Smallhampton and there's someone on a ledge below. I think they fell . . . yes, on a ledge . . . Rosie Parker . . . I think they've been there since last night . . . yes, OK, thank you.'

The voice at the other end of the line said they were going to send a helicopter out to get him. I had to stay on the phone, so I couldn't even call Ella to let her know I'd found him.

I leant over the cliff and waved down to him. 'The helicopter's coming!' I shouted. 'It's on its way!' But I don't think he heard me. The wind was taking my words and whipping them behind me.

I stayed on my knees for a few minutes, alternating between waving down to Maff and looking in the sky for the helicopter. *Hurry up!* I looked down at Maff again. He wasn't moving now. It looked like he was in a bad way. I had to get down to him, to make sure he was OK. But how? I looked to my left and realised that part of the cliff wasn't quite as steep. Luckily I was wearing my trainers with extra grip.

'Maff! I'm coming!' I shouted.

I put my mobile in my pocket and swept my hair back from my face. Then I took a deep breath and slithered backwards on my tummy so my legs were dangling over the edge. I grabbed hold of some grass and slowly moved my feet about until I found a hole for them both. Then I lowered myself down, still holding on to the grass with one hand, and found a hole for my other hand. Then I let go of the grass at the top.

I was now lying flat against the cliff face, and my chest was pounding. All I could hear was the boom-boom of my heart, and a voice in my head saying, *Don't look down! Don't look down!*

It took a long time to get to the ledge, even though it wasn't that far. I kept having to pause when I couldn't find a foothold, and take deep breaths. *You can do it, Rosie!* I kept telling myself, over and over again. I thought of Miss Osbourne, our gym teacher, always yelling at me to make an effort. If she could see me now! I tried not to think about what I was doing, and just focused on getting there. If I fell off the cliff, Soph and Abs would *kill* me!

When I was about a couple of metres away, I shouted, 'Maff?'

'Rosie! Be careful!' came the reply. He sounded very weak.

I almost cried again, hearing his voice.

I finally stepped down on to the ledge and tried to stop my legs from wobbling. Maff was lying down, shuffling along, trying to give me some room, and gasping in pain as he did so.

'Maff! We were so worried!' I said, kneeling next to him and trying to hug him. 'What happened?'

'I fell,' he said, wincing. 'I think I've broken my ankle. It really hurts.'

'You're freezing!' I said, taking off my jacket and putting it over him. 'Have you been here all night?'

'Yep,' he said, trying to smile. He was really pale, and his hair was a mess. His left foot was at a funny angle and his ankle was swollen. He flinched as I bent over his leg to look. 'My phone fell into the sea, so I couldn't call anyone.'

'Well, I've called an ambulance,' I said. 'And Steve's called the police.'

'You've met Steve?' asked Maff.

'Yup. I know your secret!' I said.

Maff looked a little uncomfortable.

'Anyway,' I said, 'we've found you now, so you're going to be fine.'

'I can't believe you climbed down here!' Maff said. 'You're amazing, Rosie!'

I blushed. Actually, I couldn't believe I'd done it either. Now I looked back up at the cliff, I was quite panicky. It was a *really* stupid thing to do. 'Well, you know . . .' I said.

'Thanks so much,' Maff said. He did a sort of half smile, but couldn't stop shivering.

Then there was this awkward silence as we stared at each other. It was a really odd situation. I was really pleased to see him, and he was really pleased to see me (although I guess he would have been pleased to see anyone at that point). But I was also totally embarrassed. I mean, I'd just shown him how much I liked him – by risking life and limb! – and I didn't know what to do next. I think he was embarrassed too. His ankle obviously really hurt, but he was trying not to show it. And he'd been rescued by a *girl*.

Where *was* that helicopter?

Maff shivered again.

'You're still cold, aren't you?' I asked.

Maff nodded. 'And hungry!' he said. 'And a bit scared. This ledge is really small.'

'Well, I can't do much about food or the ledge, but budge up.'

He moved sideways, wincing, and I sat down next to him, hugging my knees. We were squished together, which made things a bit warmer. But not much.

Now we just had to wait to be rescued.

* * *

Five minutes later, we heard the sound of a helicopter approaching. I sat up carefully and waved as it came round the corner. I looked down – *Eek!* – and saw a lot of people on the beach, standing on the rocks. They were waving. I waved back.

'Owww!' groaned Maff as he tried to sit up.

'Just stay still,' I ordered. 'Don't move!'

The helicopter was above us now, and I could see someone leaning out and waving. I waved back. It was really noisy, and the helicopter was creating loads of wind. The sea below was being churned about, and my stomach had decided to do the same thing. I clutched Maff so we wouldn't fall off the ledge. (And because I was enjoying it, I admit it!)

Then something came out of the helicopter – a man on a rope. He was slowly lowered towards us.

'Hello!' he yelled as he landed, over the sound of the whirring blades. I'd stood up, to give him room. 'I thought there was only one of you down here!'

I looked a bit sheepish.

'Well, OK, never mind. Let's get you out of here first,' he said to me. 'Then there'll be room for the stretcher. What's your name?'

'Rosie,' I shouted, over the noise. He was putting a belt and some ropes round my waist.

'I'm Phil. Grab on to me, Rosie, and we'll get you up there. Back soon, mate.'

I flung my arms round him, smiled at Maff, who was looking very worried, and the man waved at the helicopter. Then, suddenly, we were dangling in the air!

'Aaaaaaargh!!!' I screamed.

'Don't worry, you're perfectly safe!' the man shouted. It was hard to hear him in all the wind. 'Just hold on!'

He didn't need to tell *me* that. I was clinging on for dear life. We twirled round and round as we were slowly winched up towards the helicopter. It got noisier and noisier as we got nearer.

Then an arm shot out of the open door and grabbed us, hauling us in. We landed on the floor of the helicopter in a heap.

'There you go!' Phil said, unhooking me. 'Now, you just sit there and I'll go back for your friend. What's his name?'

'Maff, it's Maff. And he thinks he's broken his ankle,' I said, clambering into a seat. The man who'd pulled us in gave me a jacket to wear and then helped the first man to attach a stretcher to the cable.

'OK, we'll be back soon. Don't worry.' And he went out of the helicopter again, this time standing on the stretcher.

There was an agonising wait where I was imagining all sorts of things – Maff falling off the ledge, the stretcher banging into the cliff as it came up, the cable snapping . . .

'Don't worry. Phil is a paramedic. He'll make sure Maff's OK,' said the second bloke. 'I'm Barry, by the way. And the pilot's Clive. We've done this kind of thing lots of times before.' The pilot waved a cheery hand in my direction without looking round. I guess he had to concentrate on keeping the helicopter hovering beside the cliff.

'So, are you the girl who called us? I thought there was only one of you on the ledge?' Barry said.

'Erm, yes . . . I climbed down to check on him,' I said.

'You did *what*?!' Barry said. 'Do you know how stupid that was? You could have been killed!'

'I know,' I said, remembering the way the climb felt like it took forever and how wobbly I'd been. It had been very stupid really. I started to cry.

'You must never do anything like that again,'

Barry said, sternly. 'You should have stayed put. Didn't the person on the phone tell you that?'

Oh, yes, the person on the phone . . . I pulled my phone out of my pocket. I had ten missed calls. It must have disconnected itself from the emergency services in my pocket while I was climbing down the cliff. And I didn't hear it on the ledge cos of the wind. Oops.

'What would have happened to your friend if you'd fallen, too?' Barry continued. 'That wouldn't have helped him, would it?'

I was sobbing now. 'Sorry,' I sniffed. 'I was just really worried about him.'

'I know,' Barry said, putting his hand on my shoulder. 'Don't cry. He'll be OK. But next time you're in a situation like this, stay put!'

I nodded vigorously. *There won't* be *a next time!* I thought.

Suddenly, I saw Phil's grinning face appear from below, and then Maff's white one, all tucked up in the stretcher. He was biting his lip, trying to be brave.

Soon, Maff was safely on the helicopter floor, firmly tied to the stretcher, wincing in pain. I don't think the shuddering of the helicopter helped his ankle. But he did manage to smile at me.

'Right, off we go to hospital,' Phil said, climbing into the front of the helicopter with Clive.

'Hey, look, you're famous,' Barry said, pointing out of the side window.

As we circled round, I could see more of the beach, and there were loads more people there, looking up at the helicopter and waving. I waved back, hoping the rest of Fusion were among them. I'd done it! I'd found Maff!

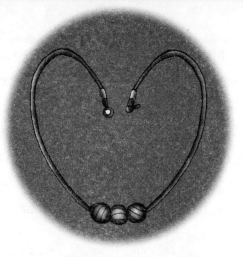

Chapter Nine

A few days later, it was time to go home. I couldn't believe the holiday had gone so quickly.

'So, I take it you're glad we came here instead of France then, Rosie?' Mum asked as she packed away her leotards. She'd only just given up telling me off for climbing down the cliff. She'd nearly had a heart attack when she'd heard what I'd done. She and Nan had been on at me about it for days. Talk about making their point! I'd totally learnt my lesson. Miss Osbourne would have to live without seeing any moments of PE brilliance from me. There was no way I was climbing up or down anything else ever again. But I did understand why Mum was so cross, and I'd tried to make it up to her. I'd helped Judy do some cleaning, as I'd promised. I'd even gone to watch the Banana Splits again. And I had to admit this had been a brilliant holiday, and I had Mum to thank for it.

'I'm very glad we came here, Mum,' I said, hugging her. 'You were right, as always.'

She laughed. 'Just remember that, young lady. Now, have you finished your packing? We have to be out of here by twelve.'

'I'm done. Can I go to the pool for a bit, please? You know, to say goodbye.'

'Off you go,' Mum said. There was a knock at the door. 'Get that, would you?'

It was the band and Jools! But not Maff. I hadn't seen him since he was released from hospital. Steve had whisked him off to his house to look after him, and Maff hadn't been back to the park. He needed to rest, apparently, and I guess it was the perfect opportunity to get to know his dad. And for his dad to meet his adoptive parents, who'd rushed down as soon as they heard what had happened. But I couldn't help wishing he'd come back. The last time I'd seen him, he'd been on a stretcher, being taken in to the hospital.

'Hi, Rosie!' Lauren yelled. 'We've come to say goodbye!'

'And to show you this,' Ella said, holding up the local paper, the *Smallhampton Times*.

'Come in, guys,' I said, taking the paper and showing them into the 'living area', where Nan was sitting, finishing her Miss Marple novel. There was a huge photo on the front page of me and Maff!!! We both looked windswept and shell-shocked, because it was taken just after we came out of the helicopter, but it was definitely us. And we were definitely holding hands!!! I couldn't wait to show the girls – and everyone at school (particularly Amanda Hawkins)!!!

'You can keep it,' Ella said, smiling. 'The article says how brave you were.'

'Thanks,' I said. 'Can't believe I'm going today!'

'I know. We're off later today, too,' Ella said. 'Look, stay in touch, won't you? You've got my number.'

'Yeah, of course! You too.' I hugged Ella. I was going to miss her.

'And here's Maff's email address,' she said quietly, slipping a piece of paper into my hand. 'I know he'd want you to stay in touch with him too.'

'Thanks,' I said. I couldn't believe I wasn't going to say goodbye to him in person. Part of me had hoped he'd be back on our last day, but it seemed he couldn't make it.

I hugged all the members of the band. They'd all been so nice – Jools had gone on for ages about how amazing it was that I'd found Maff. They hadn't been able to play the last gigs without him, so it had been a quiet few days. But everyone was just pleased he was OK – and relieved to have solved the mystery of why he kept disappearing off!

'We promise to keep up our blog, Rosie,' Sean said solemnly as he hugged me.

'You'd better!' I said.

'Take care, Rosie,' Lauren boomed. 'Don't do anything I wouldn't do.'

Nan looked up. 'That's what I always say, dear,' she said. 'Very sensible advice.'

There was the sound of coughing at the door. We all turned round. Gerry was standing there with a bunch of flowers. Nan went pink.

'Hello, Pam,' Gerry said. 'Might I have a word?'

Nan went over, putting on her raincoat, and Gerry gave her the flowers. She passed them to me and took Gerry's arm.

'We'll just take a turn around the park, Rosie,' she said. 'Tell your mum I'll be back in a bit.'

I watched as they slowly walked off. Of course, Nan had to say goodbye to someone she cared about, too. It seemed like there were going to be a lot of broken hearts today.

Mum appeared then, lugging her suitcase. Jools leapt up to help her.

'Oh, thank you,' she said. 'I don't think we've met.'

'I'm Jools,' he said, panting slightly. With the number of 'costumes' Mum's got, I'm not surprised he found it heavy.

'Oh, yes, you're the band's manager, aren't you?' Mum said.

What the crusty old grandads? 'Mum – Nan and Gerry have gone for a quick walk. Well, not that quick probably, but anyway, that's where she is. She said she'd be back soon,' I said, hoping to distract her. 'Look, he gave her these flowers.'

'They're lovely,' Mum said. 'So, Jools, you've heard of Bananarama, haven't you?'

I groaned. Jools nodded cautiously.

'Well . . .' said Mum. 'Yes, if you could put it in the boot, that would be splendid. Thank you so much. Anyway, so, as you may have heard, I do a bit of singing myself . . .' Luckily, she followed him out of the door at that point and we couldn't hear any more of that cringe-making conversation.

Five minutes later, Jools reappeared, looking

rather harassed, with Mum. She looked a bit disappointed.

'Right, come on then, Rosie,' she said briskly. 'We need to hand in our keys.'

This was it. The end of the holiday. And no Maff. I sighed, and then hugged the band again. We all went outside and Mum locked up.

Nan and Gerry came walking down the path.

'Goodbye then, sweet Pam,' Gerry said, kissing her hand. 'I hope to speak to you soon.'

'Indeed,' Nan giggled.

Gerry held the car door open for her and she climbed in. I got in the back and Mum started the engine.

'Bye!' yelled Lauren and Ella, waving.

I waved back. 'Bye!'

'Enjoy Bananarama!' Sean shouted wickedly.

And we were off. Back to boring Borehurst, where no hot band members lived. I sighed.

We were just approaching the gates of the holiday park – my heart sinking lower and lower – when a car sped towards us. It started flashing its lights and honking the horn at us.

'Mum! Pull over!' I shouted. Whoever it was, they were in a hurry.

Mum stopped on the side of the road and the other car stopped too. Then the back door opened and Maff got out!!! He had his ankle in plaster, so he was wobbling about, trying to get his crutches out of the car. Then he hopped over towards us.

'Well, go on then, Rosie,' said Nan. 'Go and say goodbye!'

I got out of the car and ran over to him, flinging my arms around him.

'I thought I was going to miss you!' Maff said, leaning on me for balance. 'I kept telling Steve to drive faster!'

'I'm so glad you came,' I said.

'Listen, I've got something for you,' he said. He reached around his neck and took off his Mexican necklace. 'I want you to have it.'

'Really?' *Wow*! He *never* took that off.

'Yeah. I mean, it's just a little thing. You saved my life after all!' he joked.

I blushed. 'Thank you.' I put the necklace on.

'I'll never forget you, Rosie. What you did for me . . . that was amazing.' Maff put his arms around me. 'Look, I'm going home this afternoon, so I'll email you tonight, OK?'

'OK,' I whispered.

'I really want to stay in touch with you,' he said.

And then he kissed me!!! It was really soft, and really gentle, and really amazing!! When we stopped, I didn't know what to say.

Then Mum beeped the horn. Honestly, how to ruin a romantic moment! Oh – quelle horreur!! I'd just realised she and Nan and Steve had all seen my first kiss!!! Très embarrassing! I went red.

'I'd better go,' I blurted.

Maff nodded. 'Speak to you soon, Nosy Parker,' he said.

I got back into the car and caught Mum's eye in the mirror. 'Don't say anything,' I said.

Nan was humming. 'What a nice boy,' she said.

Yes, he was a nice boy. And he'd kissed me!!! I had to text the girls:

Me: On way home now. LOADS 2 tell u!!!

Abs: Can't WAIT 2 c u!!! We've miiissed u!!! How's the hottie?!?!

Me: He's sooo lovely!! :-))) Will spill the beans when i c u . . .

Abs: Ooh, beans to spill – sounds très exciting!!

Me: You bet – get ready for a marathon goss sesh!!! ;-) X

Fact File

NAME: Soph (Sophie) McCoy

AGE: 14

STAR SIGN: Pisces

HAIR: Long, wavy and dark brown

EYES: Brown

LOVES: Getting compliments for another cool, customised creation

HATES: Wearing anything that isn't mega-stylish

LAST SEEN: Rummaging along the charity shop rails to find the finishing touches to her latest funky fashions

MOST LIKELY TO SAY: 'You can laugh now, but you'll all be wearing this in six months' time'

WORST CRINGE EVER: Once she turned up at a sleepover with her mum's pyjamas instead of hers! She'll never live down having to wear those hideous flowered PJs!

Megastar

Everyone has blushing blunders - here are some from your Megastar Mysteries friends!

Maff

I was on stage, singing my heart out, when suddenly I felt something really wrong in my stomach. I thought I was going to be sick, so I had to run off as fast as I could. I was in such a hurry that I forgot I was still carrying my guitar. I ended up catching my leg on the lead and tumbling head first off stage and straight into the crowd! Sooo not cool!

Ella

I'd managed to wangle an audition with a really cool band and I was desperate to impress them. I dressed up in my most rockin' outfit, grabbed my guitar from my bedroom floor and got to the audition as fast as I could. When I arrived I was so nervous I just wanted to get it over with. I opened up my guitar case, grabbed the guitar, then noticed there was a pair of pink pants caught in the strings! I was très embarrassed! Luckily, the band thought it was so funny they wrote a song about it!

Cringes

Soph

I was on my hols in France when I spotted a really cool clothes shop and just had to go inside. I tried on loads of outfits and found the sweetest little vest top. I totally had to buy it. I paid and headed out, only for the alarm to go off, making even more noise than Abs' little sister! The next thing I know this French security guard was trying to march me to the police station! Luckily, Abs arrived and was able to show him that I had actually paid for my item! Such a nightmare and really embarrassing!

Lauren

When I was younger, the only thing I ever wanted for Christmas was a set of drums cos I was desperate to start playing. Every year I'd ask for them but they'd never arrive. Then, one year, I finally got them and as soon as I'd opened them I started banging about, making tons of noise. I got so into it that I started twirling my sticks in the air and, as I did, I managed to chuck them up and they smashed straight into the TV! The screen smashed and my dad grounded me for ages! Eek!

Be the BEST Best Mate

These top tips will keep you and your friend mates for life!

1 ALWAYS LISTEN to your mate, unless she's trying to convince you that dressing head to toe in orange is actually a really good idea.

2 DON'T TELL anyone else her secrets, unless you want everyone to know all those dodgy things she knows about you!

3 SHARE THINGS, whether it's celeb gossip, clothes or secrets. Having a best mate is all about having fun together.

4 REMEMBER TO MAKE UP if you argue. Good mates are hard to find, so try and keep hold of her!

5 DON'T BE JOINED AT THE HIP. If you're together 24-7 then what will you have to talk about? Join clubs and try new things, that way there's lots more to gossip about!

6 BE DIFFERENT. If she's obsessed with fashion and you love reading then you can learn loads of new things from each other.

7 HAVE A LAUGH. Mates who giggle together have loads more chance of still being best friends when they're old and grey!

8 BE HONEST. Tell her if you're upset and you can sort it out together!

9 TELL HER SHE'S FAB. Make her a cute card or just tell her in person, it'll make her feel awesome!

10 BE YOURSELF. If you want to be mates for life then you have to stay true to yourself, after all, what's not to like about someone as cool as you?!

YOUR GUIDE TO MUM-SPEAK

Here's our guide to what your mum says, and what she really means . . .

Mum says:	What she really means:
Not today, love	Not ever – it's never going to happen!
I'm not really sure . . .	Give me five minutes to think of an excuse!
Well . . .	You're really not going to like this!
I'll just be a minute	Make that an hour!
Have you finished your dinner?	I spent hours slaving over a hot stove and you didn't even eat it!
Could you turn it down?	Your music sounds worse that a cat clawing a blackboard!
That's nice, darling	I've no idea what you're saying because there's something good on the telly!
Oooh, he's cute	He's just like a young George Clooney!
Well, in my day . . .	I was just as much of a nightmare, but I'm not telling you that!
How much?	You'd think it would be made of gold for that price!

Who's Your Fusion Friend?

Find out who'd be your band bestie!

1. You love to spend your Saturdays . . .
a. Writing songs
b. Hitting the shops
c. Reading in your room
d. Playing your CDs very, very loudly!

2. What would be your dream birthday party?
a. Recording a single in a studio
b. Having a sleepover in your fave shop
c. Heading to your fave restaurant
d. Going to a pop concert

3. Your hair is . . .
a. Always cool, it's naturally that way
b. Short and easy to look after
c. A bit of a mess!
d. Pretty different . . .

4. At school, what's your fave subject?
a. English, you love writing stories
b. Art, being creative rocks
c. Maths, you love solving problems
d. Drama, you wanna be noticed

5. What do you dream of doing in the future?

a. Being a world-famous pop star
b. Running your own fashion mag
c. Being a famous author
d. Acting in your fave soap

6. What do your friends come to you for?

a. Cool CDs to borrow
b. Amazing fashion tips
c. Help with homework
d. A girlie giggle

How did you score?

Mostly As: Maff
You and Maff would be best friends cos you're obsessed with music and you could spend all your time going to gigs, listening to CDs and being your own band!

Mostly Bs: Ella
Ella would be your perfect best mate cos you could share clothes, swap style tips and have tons of mega sleepovers! You'd be the prettiest band, ever!

Mostly Cs: Sean
You and Sean have tons in common cos you're quiet, sweet and always thinking of others! You two would watch movies, read books and do well at school!

Mostly Ds: Lauren
Lauren and you would be mates cos you're fun, daring and ready for anything! You'd be busy playing jokes, being loud and having a great time!

Soph's Style Tips

SPARKLY STAR

What you need: gems, fabric glue

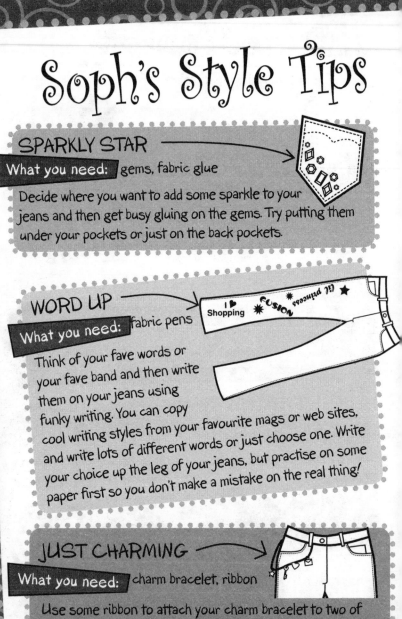

Decide where you want to add some sparkle to your jeans and then get busy gluing on the gems. Try putting them under your pockets or just on the back pockets.

WORD UP

What you need: fabric pens

Think of your fave words or your fave band and then write them on your jeans using funky writing. You can copy cool writing styles from your favourite mags or web sites, and write lots of different words or just choose one. Write your choice up the leg of your jeans, but practise on some paper first so you don't make a mistake on the real thing!

JUST CHARMING

What you need: charm bracelet, ribbon

Use some ribbon to attach your charm bracelet to two of your belt loops and dangle it between them to make a cute key chain.

Jazz up your old jeans with Soph's customising cool!

RIBBON RULES

What you need: ribbon, fabric glue, scissors

Cut the ribbon into strips, then glue the strips from the hem of your jeans up. Make them different lengths for a funky look.

FABRIC FUN

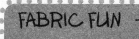

What you need: Funky fabric, fabric glue, scissors

Cut the fabric so it covers one of your back pockets. Then glue it on to your pocket for an easy makeover! You could even use material from an old top to make this a mega-cheap make!

SWIRLY GIRLY

What you need: fabric pens, plain paper

Practise drawing some swirly lines on your paper first and then draw super-swirly lines under each of your front pockets for a funky look.

The Wheel of DESTINY

WHAT TO DO:

Look at the Wheel of Destiny and hold your finger above it.

Close your eyes and drop your finger on to the wheel.

Open your eyes, see what number you landed on and read what could be happening soon . . .

NUMBER 1

A new friend could bring you a cool surprise! Your lucky colour is blue, so wear it with pride!

NUMBER 2

Put on a happy face and smile at everyone today. The number two could be very lucky for you . . .

NUMBER 3

Good things come in threes, so look out for lovely stuff heading your way very, very soon!

NUMBER 4

It's time to try something new and see what happens. Who knows where you could end up!

NUMBER 5

A journey to somewhere new could bring you a great new mate and wear lots of green for luck!

NUMBER 6

Being nice will bring you lots of really fab things. Try it and see how cool your life can be!

NUMBER 7

Animals are lucky for you, so spend some time with one and get ready for tons of fab things!

NUMBER 8

Trying a new look could get you noticed, and who knows what amazing things could happen next!

NUMBER 9

Be confident and wear your fave necklace to give yourself lots of happy days!

Pam's Problem Page

Never fear, Pam's here to sort you out!

Dear Pam,

I dream of becoming a mega-famous rock star and travelling the world, performing my music to thousands of screaming fans. How can I make my dreams become a reality?

Maff

Pam says: Oooh, a rock star, you say? Would that be like that Cliff Richard chap? I do like him and I think he'd be lovely to share a cup of tea and a garibaldi with. We never did any of this music malarkey in my day. Why don't you just find a nice young lady and try working in a bank or something? That could be very exciting — you could tuck into custard creams during your tea breaks. If you really want to be famous then how about doing something really important like becoming an actor. You could help Inspector Morse solve some crimes . . .

Can't wait for the next
book in the series?
Here's a sneak preview of

Gemini

AVAILABLE NOW
from all good bookshops, or
www.mega-star.co.uk

PRODUCTION *Gemini*

DIRECTOR *Robert D. Squire*

DATE *03/04*

SCENE *Big Night Out*

TAKE *17*

CAMERA *Greg*

Chapter One

I owe Soph's Aunt Penny, big time! And I'm talking SERIOUSLY big time – not just, like, the favour you owe your mate who distracted the teacher so you didn't have to answer that awkward question. No, Penny is très marvelloso with sequins on top. Basically, she totally rocks! Firstly, she's nice and always talks to me, Soph and Abs like we're normal people, not annoying kids (even though Soph drives her mad, asking about the latest fashion goss). Secondly, she looks like a rock star with her skinny jeans and cool T-shirts.

Thirdly, she is a fashion stylist and knows EVERYONE there is to know. And finally, most importantly, she's styling Australia's most famous and gorgeous teen actresses, the Sweetland twins, on their first film, which is being shot in London. Oh, yes, and SHE'S GOT ME, ABS AND SOPH JOBS AS RUNNERS ON THE SET!!!

As soon as we heard that Penny was going to be working on the film, about a month before Easter, Soph started begging her to get us on set somehow. We knew it was a long shot, but as Abs pointed out, the opportunity to meet megastars like the Sweetlands doesn't tend to come along regularly. Every day we'd ask Soph for news and every day she'd shake her head sadly. 'Penny said she'd see what she can do,' was the best she could manage.

And then, the evening after school broke up for Easter, when we were all looking forward to a long holiday filled with mad family members and wandering round boring old Borehurst, Soph instant-messaged me and Abs:

FashionPolice: Guess what!!!

CutiePie: You've come up with a new smock design and Topshop are going to stock it?

FashionPolice: Oh, ha, ha. Very funny, Abs. You wait – one day I will *rule* the fashion shelves. Or rails. Whatever. Anyway, guess again.

NosyParker: Meanie Greenie rang you up and said, actually, don't do all that homework this holiday, Soph. And tell Abs and Rosie not to bother either.

FashionPolice: Nope. Penny rang and said we could go on the set!!!

NosyParker: YOU LIE!!!

FashionPolice: Au contraire, mon frère. And it's even better than that!

CutiePie: What could be better than going on a film set and meeting the Sweetland twins?!

FashionPolice: We'll be there for two weeks. She's got us jobs as runners!!!

NosyParker: AAAAAAAAAAAAAAAAAAAA AAAAAAAAAAAAAAAAAAAARGH!
CutiePie: AAAAAAAAAAAAAAAAAAAA AAAAAAAAAAAAAAAAAARGH!

Imagine – two weeks on a film set! This was so going to be the best Easter holiday ever!

While I was doing a victory dance in my bedroom, Nan popped her head round the door.

'You all right, Rosie love?' she asked. 'There's a heck of a lot of banging about going on.'

'Nan! I'm going to be a runner!!!' I shrieked, grabbing her hands and trying to get her to do a jig with me. 'How cool is that?'

'A runner? But I thought you hated PE?' Nan said, confused.

I burst out giggling. Who cared about anything else – I was going to be working in the film industry!

* * *

And now we were on the train on the way to Penny's flat, accompanied by Soph's mum. Soph had my copy of *Star Secrets* magazine and was testing me on my knowledge of the twins. I buy *Star Secrets* every week and what I don't know about most celebs isn't worth knowing. If only there were a lesson at school where I could apply this knowledge. But no, we have to stick to boring old maths and French and the like. Yawn-o-rama.

'OK, so what's Paige's favourite colour?' Soph asked me.

'Blue,' I replied, rolling my eyes at the easy-peasiness of the question.

'What was the name of Shelby's first crush?' asked Abs, peering at the quiz over Soph's shoulder.

'Jonathan Appleby,' I said.

'Their characters' middle names in *Hart Grove*?' Soph said.

'Amy and Kate,' I crowed.

'Their star sign?'

'Gemini – duh!'

'OK, OK, we give up. You know everything there is to know about Paige and Shelby

Sweetland,' Abs sighed.

'Yes! I told you I did!' I punched the air with glee. Abs made a big 'loser' sign at me.

'Girls!' said Soph's mum, looking round the train carriage with embarrassment. She had volunteered to escort us to London, but I think she was regretting it. 'Remember what Aunt Penny said – you've got to treat them like ordinary people.'

'Yeah, OK, Mum,' Soph said. 'But they're not ordinary, are they? I mean, *ordinary* people don't star in a soap opera their whole lives!'

'*Ordinary* people don't star in their own film when they're only sixteen!' Abs pointed out.

Mrs McCoy rolled her eyes. 'Remember, you're there to do a job. Don't go all starry-eyed – you'll put Penny in a difficult position. She stuck her neck out to get you these runner jobs, so you've got to work hard.'

'We know, Mum!' Soph said. 'We'll be good. Although I don't know about Rosie. She always starts babbling rubbish when we meet celebrities.'

'I do not!' I protested. 'Well, OK, I do some-times. But you make it sound as if we meet them all the time. Which we don't.'

'Unlike Penny,' said Soph enviously. 'I'm so going to be a stylist before I become a designer – you get to meet *everyone*.'

'Don't forget that *we've* met Mirage Mullins, who's a proper megastar number-one chart sensation,' Abs pointed out. 'And Rosie's got Maff from Fusion's number . . .'

I went red. It was true. Maff – the lead singer of a totally cool band – had been my first kiss. He's totally gorge *and* a pop star! In fact, since we'd last seen one another, Fusion had got into the Top 40 – so he was totally famous too!

'It's not like he's my boyfriend,' I said.

'Only in your dreams,' Soph sighed. Seriously, sometimes Soph is so soppy, it's worrying.

Mrs McCoy sighed too. She was getting embarrassed by us being noisy (she actually has a sense of what is embarrassing and what isn't, unlike some mothers I could mention), but honestly, I don't know how she expected us to be quiet and sensible. Obviously, normally we were nice, well-behaved girls, a credit to our parents and our school – well, mostly. But hello?? We were going to meet Paige and Shelby Sweetland!!! The only thing that could have made it better was if Amanda Hawkins, our arch-enemy from school, had known about it. It would have been seriously good to have spent the whole last day at school being very, very smug. But it would be even better to tell her about it after we had met them. I couldn't wait to see Amanda's face after the Easter holidays!

'What do runners do, anyway?' I asked.

'Oh, just run messages and stuff about. You know, be helpful on the set,' Abs said knowledgeably.

'Ah. I can do that. I'm good at that,' I said. Imagine, I was going to meet the Sweetland twins – maybe even become their friend – and all I had to do was be helpful! This was going to be good.

Just then, the train driver announced we were coming into the station. London, here we come!

I am so planning to live in London when I become a top celebrity reporter. Penny's flat was coolissimo! It was really small, but it had amazing views of the city and she'd decorated it really nicely – loads of cream furniture and funky accessories. It looked like it was straight out of a magazine. Abs, Soph and I were going to share the spare room, for two whole weeks!! Good old Soph – her powers of persuasion were just getting better and better. One day, she might even convince my nan to wear one of her fashion creations.

When we arrived, Soph's mum and Penny had a cup of tea and a chat, while me, Abs and Soph ran from room to room, imagining it was our flat and we all lived there together. We made a pact to live together when Soph is a fashion queen, like her aunt, and I'm a celeb reporter and Abs is . . . well, whatever she wants to be! That's something I love about her – she's so brainy. She says she's currently keeping her options open. I think she'd make a good detective. Or maybe prime minister.

Before Mrs McCoy left, she made each of us promise about a million times to be good and do what Penny told us and not get into any trouble – over and over again – while we nodded. As soon as the door closed behind her, we sat Penny down to ask her about Paige and Shelby.

'Is it true they can read each other's minds?' I asked.

'What? No!' Penny laughed.

'Oh. Well, what are they like? Are they really snobby?' asked Soph.

Before Penny could answer, Abs jumped in. 'I reckon they're really nice. They always seem down to earth in interviews. But is it hard to tell them apart?'

'Do they choose their own clothes?' Soph asked.

'Well –' Penny began.

'I can't believe we're going to meet them!' I squealed.

'I know! This is the best Easter ever!' Soph and

Abs said at exactly the same time. Well, it was!

'Girls, girls, calm down,' said Penny. 'Now, I know you're really excited, but you've got to play it cool. Paige and Shelby *are* very nice and you should treat them as ordinary people, not huge stars. They're just teenagers like you, you know.'

'I sooo believe you,' Soph said, wide-eyed and innocent.

'Well, they are! And when you're on set, remember that you're at the bottom of the ladder, and you must do whatever anyone asks you to do – and quickly.'

'Just like my Saturday job at the salon,' Soph said, nodding. She worked every weekend at the Dream Beauty salon, but she'd taken time off over Easter to be on the film set.

'You'll probably have to do things like get coffees and take memos around the set and so on. Remember the three Ps: be polite, be punctual and be personable.'

We looked blankly at Penny. Person-*what?*

'Personable means friendly,' Penny smiled.

'Film sets are fun, but people will get cross with you if you get in the way.'

'No problemo. You'll hardly know we're there,' Abs said. 'So how big an entourage do Paige and Shelby have?'

Penny shrugged. 'I don't know – there are quite a few people working for them. I'm their stylist, of course. And they have a hairdresser. They've even got their own astrologer!'

'Really?' I asked. 'Someone tells them their horoscope every day?'

'Yes,' Penny said. 'They're really into all that.'

'Hey, what does Destiny Blake say for Pisces this week?' Soph said.

I flicked to the horoscopes page in *Star Secrets* to read what their astrologer had predicted. 'You will meet new people, so stay open to new experiences. And give your friends your last bit of chocolate.'

'Oh, ha, ha,' Soph said, grabbing *Star Secrets* from me. 'Well, Sagittarians should watch out for trouble coming their way apparently. So that's you warned if you nick my chocolate.'

'I wonder if any other celeb has a personal astrologer?' Abs said.

'I can't think of anyone,' I mused. Then I gasped. 'They're setting a new trend – right under our noses!'

'Soon no one will be able to do anything without consulting their astrologer! There'll be chaos in celeb world if anything happens to the stargazers!' Abs said.

'Hmm,' Penny said. 'Well, Paige and Shelby's astrologer is certainly influential. They listen to everything she says. Not that that's always a good idea.'

'Why? What do you mean?' I asked.

'Oh, nothing. Just that she seems to have quite a hold on their careers. They hardly make a decision without her. It's a shame, because they're clever girls and they can think for themselves. After all, they've been in the business for years. But their astrologer's a bit odd sometimes.'

'Really?' I breathed. 'Does she make them stay in bed every Friday the thirteenth and stuff like that?'

'Oh, I don't know really,' Penny said, suddenly

looking a bit edgy. 'Anyway, I shouldn't be saying all this. It's very unprofessional of me. And please don't go on about how weird it is to the twins. They're a bit sensitive about her.' Penny checked her amazingly cool diver's watch. 'Oh, look at the time. Right, girls, we've got a very early start. We've got to be on set at six-thirty, and I imagine you want some beauty sleep.'

'We're about to meet two of the most beautiful teen stars in the world. Of *course* we want some beauty sleep!' Soph said. 'And I've got to decide what to wear!'

'Good grief. Right, we definitely need to get to bed now then!' Penny said, winking at Abs and me.

'Last one in bed's a Z-list celeb,' I shouted, running to the bathroom.

'Night, girls!' Penny called.

Tomorrow we were going to meet Paige and Shelby Sweetland! I couldn't wait!